LINEAGE
and Other Stories

by

Bo Lozoff

human kindness foundation   *   durham, nc

© Human Kindness Foundation 1988

Fifteenth Printing: 2018 (290,000 copies in print)
all rights reserved
ISBN 978-0-9614444-1-9
Library of Congress Catalog Card # 88-82755
printed in the U.S.A.

Cover art: Luis Suave Gonzalez
Cover design: Joshua Lozoff
Back cover photograph: Steven Ray Miller

Copies of this book are sent free to incarcerated people throughout the world. Human Kindness Foundation is a non-profit organization which sponsors the Prison-Ashram Project and other programs promoting basic kindness and spiritual sanity. 100% of the proceeds from book sales and your donations go to support these programs. For more information, write:

Human Kindness Foundation
PO Box 61619
Durham, NC 27715

Or visit our website at: www.humankindness.org

Other books by Bo Lozoff:

Available free to people who are incarcerated:

WE'RE ALL DOING TIME (1985) — also published in Spanish and Dutch; previously published in French and Italian.

JUST ANOTHER SPIRITUAL BOOK (1990)

DEEP & SIMPLE (1999)

We re sorry, we re not able to send the following books for free:

IT'S A MEANINGFUL LIFE: IT JUST TAKES PRACTICE (2000)

Bo s beautifully illustrated children s books:
THE WONDERFUL LIFE OF A FLY WHO COULDN'T FLY (2002)
A LITTLE BOY IN THE LAND OF RHYME (2011)

Table Of Contents

In Loving Memory

Bo Lozoff died on November 29, 2012, in a motorcycle accident. He is deeply missed. We are grateful to be able to continue sharing his writings.

—Human Kindness Foundation
2013

THE SADDEST BUDDHA

THE SADDEST BUDDHA

Bhikku Anatto entered noiselessly and kneeled on the straw mat directly opposite the Achaan. He marveled at the elderly man's serenity. The Achaan sat, eyes lightly closed, with a tenderness of countenance which can only come from making peace with the countless forms of suffering human beings may experience.

Bhikku Anatto closed his eyes also and assumed a meditative posture with his back, neck and head in a straight line and his lower abdomen protruding ever so slightly in order to create a firm center of balance. The two men sat, two gentle presences resting harmlessly on the Earth as it continued turning around the sun, two silent wayfarers on a timeless journey into the Great Mystery. Elsewhere on the same small planet, all the greed and sorrow, fear and violence, war and famine, pollution and self-destruction continued unabated, as it always had. But there in a humble *wat*, or monastery, in the anonymous jungles of Thailand, life made sense. There was peace. Or at least, for Bhikku Anatto, the promise of peace.

"Your practice is strong?"

Bhikku Anatto was startled by the Achaan's voice. The weekly interview had begun. He opened his eyes and looked directly into the kindly, bottomless black eyes of his teacher.

"Yes, Bhante."

The elder sat perfectly still, looking past the eyes into the soul of the young American bhikku -- monk -- across from him. His expression gradually took on a lovingly skeptical look, almost mischievous, as if to say, "oh, yeah?"

Bhikku Anatto began to glance uncomfortably around the room, over the achaan's head, down at his own feet -- everywhere but into the old man's eyes.

"Very well, then, Bhikku Anatto, you may go."

Damn!, the young bhikku lamented to himself as he neared his thatched-roofed *kuti* in the jungle. He had so deeply wanted to open up this time, so passionately wanted to blurt out his pain and confusion, to cry and be consoled, to scream his countless doubts and be reassured that he would indeed attain the peace he so desperately sought. Now he would have to endure another full week of silence before his next opportunity.

Silence. Hah! What a joke. The more quiet his environment, the more clearly Bhikku Anatto became aware of the ceaseless pandemonium which was called his mind. *Silence indeed.* Silence of mind was what he sought, certainly, but he felt no closer to it here, as an ordained bhikku, than he did as Michael Cohen, aimlessly wandering the noisy streets of New York, L.A., Paris or Morocco, trying in vain to annihilate his horrible guilt through drugs. It still amazed him that he had agreed to accompany Noelle to Thailand for a meditation course, and it absolutely stupefied him that he stayed on after the course and took ordination vows.

Bitterly, Bhikku Anatto picked up his beggar's bowl and trod perfunctorily in the direction of the village for his daily alms round. Along the path, he felt embarrassed when villagers saluted him, greeting him with reverence as one who had renounced their mundane world of desires, fears, and ambitions. He felt like a foreigner and a fraud, playing monk as a child might play dress-up in his father's business suit. Alms rounds always made him uncomfortable anyway, as he hadn't yet been able to shed his Western associations of begging and panhandling.

"Things are very different here," Bhikku Piyavanno, one of the senior monks, had tried to explain to him on his first alms rounds three months earlier. "The villagers understand that what we do, we are doing for them as well as for ourselves. They are honored to feed us."

Bhikku Anatto had looked blankly back, so the middle-aged man continued, in his halting English, "Renouncing world for life of reflection is ultimate act of compassion. You see it as retreat or escape, and therefore as act of selfishness. So you feel guilty receiving gift of food because you do not share labor. But this is not true state of things. The villagers understand, and you do not understand."

"They understand a monk's labor is more difficult than any other -- conquering mind, breaking through illusions of time and space, of life and death. They are in awe and gratitude when they see you approach. They thank you for reminding them that all their suffering is illusion. The sight of your robes alone reminds them of Buddha's victory over all suffering. It is same as Christian's gratitude that Christ achieved salvation for all of us. Buddha and Christ, they are same awareness. Conquest over suffering, and salvation for all mankind -- they are same achievement."

Bhikku Anatto surely understood intellectually; in fact he was excited and encouraged by this idea of conquest over suffering more than anything else he had ever learned. But in his gut, he was still Michael Cohen, now with a shaved head and dressed in a funny orange robe, panhandling food every day from people whose lifetime income probably wouldn't equal what he had spent on his prom night in New York City. Maybe Bhikku Piyavanno was doing it for them, but Michael/Anatto certainly wasn't. He didn't really know why he was doing anything anymore. That's what impelled him to stay in the wat in the first place.

And in three months' time, he hadn't yet summoned the courage to tell any of his teachers about the wreck. But now his nightmares were beginning again, and as a monk he had no hash or pot to defeat them.

By the time Bhikku Anatto completed his alms rounds, he had made the decision to break protocol and burst in on the Achaan without waiting for his next scheduled interview. *I can't take this for another week. He'll understand. God, please let him understand, and not kick me out.*

Bhikku Anatto's resolve mounted and his pace quickened gradually along the entire three-mile path, so that by the time he arrived at the wat he was practically in a run, doing his clumsy best to guide his bare feet around rocks and twigs, and nearly tripping over his robes as he hurried to the achaan's kuti. To the native Thai monks who watched that spectacle, such uncurbed emotional chaos and spontaneity were not an unprecedented sight, but an invariably American one. They smiled behind Bhikku Anatto's back as an older brother might smile at the various rites of passage a teenager has to endure, so serious and painful at the time, and merely a passing chuckle by the time each teen year is over.

Huffing and puffing, Bhikku Anatto tried to collect himself for a moment before knocking on the door. *Yeah, this is right. I mean, rules aren't everything, anyway. How can any of us schedule our big breakthroughs? Maybe this is an important moment for me, and it's an act of courage to face the achaan spontaneously. In fact, how else could we develop courage if we never broke the rules? That's probably the reason they make so many rules!*

Courage and rationalization both on shaky ground, he rapped lightly on the flimsy bamboo door. But the door, hung in place with only jute hinges and a jute latch, gave slightly with each knock, resulting in no knock at all, just a slight push inward with each stroke. *Oh great! If I knock any harder, I might just push it all the way open. I can just hear it now: "Crazy American busts down door, barges violently in on Bhante."*

After a moment's pause, Bhikku Anatto held the door shut with his right hand and tried knocking a little harder with his left. He achieved a little sound, but there was no response from within. Frustration mounting and courage fast waning, he held tighter and rapped harder. Still no response. By now he had become so obsessed, he hadn't noticed Bhikku Piyavanno standing just a few feet off to the side, watching with a monk's calm and patience, plus perhaps a little bit of restraint in order to avoid smiling. Of all the monks in residence, Bhikku Piyavanno was the only one allowed to speak whenever he deemed it necessary for the proper functioning of the wat.

"Achaan is not inside. He has gone into retreat."

Bhikku Anatto was startled and embarrassed.

"But, but I really need to see him. I mean, my interview was just this morning, and well, I mean, uh,..."

In a reassuring voice and a carefree smile which made him look almost like a dolphin, Bhikku Piyavanno simply repeated, "He has gone into retreat." Then he added, with polite reproach, "Please do not break vow of silence, Bhikku."

Bhikku Anatto leaned against the door frame in despair.

Bhikku Piyavanno continued, "You must go into retreat now, too. For one week. The Achaan has selected a cave for you, a few miles from here. A friend is coming from village to guide you through jungle."

Bhikku Anatto looked at Piyavanno with near-panic in his eyes. His first impulse was to scream, *Fuck you! I can't take this shit anymore.* But then where would he go? What would he do? Suicide would be the only answer. And, of course, his "suicide reasoning," which convinced him to ordain as a monk in the first place, still made sense: *Well, I may as well try this first. I can always kill myself later if it doesn't work out.*

On the long walk to his retreat cave, Bhikku Anatto's local guide talked nearly non-stop, as villagers often did in the presence of silent monks. Bhikku Anatto's grasp of the Thai language was very basic, but surprisingly he felt he caught the villager's drift. There was something about being a Communist, yet retaining a reverence for Buddhism and for monks. Then there was something about guerrilla forays over the Vietnamese border, and there was also something about Americans -- not angry, exactly, but perhaps stymied more than anything else, about their ignorant, self-centered intrusions into the politics of third-world nations.

The cave was beautiful, like a hidden jewel set deep within the jungle. Airy and bright, it was kept very clean by the monks who used it for retreat. Its mouth was no more than eight feet across but it was at least six feet high as well, and Bhikku Anatto was relieved that he didn't have to stoop way over and half crawl through a long passage as he had done in another cave the previous month. The dirt floor, about a hundred square feet of space, was spotlessly swept. The cave was entirely empty except for a grass broom, a bamboo mat and a water pot, and about three feet high, on a makeshift shelf which had been carved out of the hard mud wall, a small supply of candles and matches.

Bhikku Anatto's mood brightened slightly as he looked around at such natural beauty and simplicity. *There's gotta be something to all of this. Look at this; this doesn't come out of chaos and madness. There's gotta be something to it.* He felt a small, contented smile creep upon his face, and realized that at that moment, he must indeed have looked like a monk to the earnest young man who had led him there.

His guide pointed out the stream and fruit trees, a crude jungle latrine and a small but steady waterfall which was the safest source of drinking water. He showed Bhikku Anatto the proper tree -- a relative of American sassafras -- from which to acquire fragrant, pliable young branches to use as disposable toothbrushes. Finally, he said something which Bhikku Anatto translated roughly as "Better not try to return to the monastery before I come back next week, because you'll be one lost, sorry son of a bitch in this trackless jungle." Whatever the exact words, he certainly conveyed that drift.

Then Bhikku Anatto was alone in the magnificent jungle, like being held prisoner in the Garden of Eden. He tried to delight in the sounds of countless birds singing, distant bands of monkeys chattering away, and the fresh scents of wild ginger, ripe mangoes and the many unknown but distinct jungle fragrances served to his senses by a moist, gentle breeze. But he felt sadness beginning its recurring effort to take over his heart and mind; sadness and the terrible, terrifying aloneness which always brought with it ideas of suicide.

No! I'm a bhikku, and I'm going to do my practice. I refuse to be held in slavery by uncontrolled emotions.

He entered the cave with proper reverence and firmly placed his small, maroon cloth bag next to the bamboo mat, and sat in meditation. He focused all his attention on his breath as it flowed endlessly in and out, in and out, defining his life itself. As he had been instructed, he noticed every sensation, thought and feeling, striving not to cling to or expand upon them. He reflected on the teachings he had received.

Just notice, and return to the breath. Notice, and return to the breath. Awareness follows control. Awareness follows concentration. Learn to focus on present reality, the most basic present reality such as your own breath, and you will discover your latent awareness of all wisdom. Enlightenment is neither gained nor acquired; it is neither bestowed nor received; the Buddha Nature is discovered as your own simplest awareness, the awareness which you have always possessed and which can never be destroyed.

Bhikku Anatto sat for an hour or so, not his best or worst meditation, and then lay down as the sun began to set over the far cliffs. What a constant struggle it was, striving so hard to open and clear his mind, yet simultaneously trying to keep in check the latent flood of emotions surrounding the wreck. His battle seemed to be getting harder rather than easier, as if meditation practice was reducing his ability to distract himself rather than helping him to transcend such thoughts and memories, as

14

he had hoped. Exhausted from his confusion and long journey into the jungle, he at last fell asleep.

It was dark when he awoke, and Bhikku Anatto had no idea whether it was the middle of the night or close to dawn. When he couldn't get back to sleep, he stood and felt his way along the wall until his hand -- which he hoped against hope wouldn't surprise any giant spiders -- reached the shelf which held candles and matches. He lit a candle and placed it on the center front edge of the shelf, taking care to isolate it enough from the other candles and matches that they wouldn't all ignite and doom him to darkness for his remaining nights in the cave.

With the candle flickering gently, casting slightly frightening shadows all around him, Bhikku Anatto started toward the mouth of the cave to take a few deep breaths of fresh night air, but froze in his tracks as he noticed that one of the shadows was three-dimensional. Focusing his vision even as his blood turned cold and the hair stood up on the back of his neck, the young bhikku beheld the largest snake he had ever seen, in or out of captivity. (Actually, he only beheld half of the largest snake he had ever seen, but his imagination assured him that the tail end which disappeared into a cranny of the cave wall was every bit as large as the head end which lay directly between himself and the only exit.)

In point of fact it was an undeniably large boa constrictor, about fifteen feet long and at least six inches in diameter. A boa of similar dimensions had been autopsied a few years earlier in India and found to have died from internal injuries which had resulted from swallowing a gazelle. Whole.

Michael David Cohen Bhikku Anatto had never

imagined, let alone experienced, such fear. He could smell fear pervading the entire cave, he could see fear rippling through the candlelight between himself and the snake, he could hear fear crashing like a thousand waterfalls echoing ceaselessly from wall to wall. He couldn't scream or move. His heart felt as if it would explode any moment, pounding so hard it took his breath away. Nothing in the universe existed except the bhikku and the snake -- mostly the snake.

After some time frozen in place, Bhikku Anatto found himself backing up, almost imperceptibly slowly, and crumpling down on the mat with his back against the cave wall. It must have taken twenty minutes to move those four or five feet. His eyes hadn't wandered or even blinked in all that time. Although it was a warm October night, he was bone-shaking, knee-knocking freezing as he kept his vigil for what seemed like centuries.

In time, Bhikku Anatto regained enough reasonability to notice that the boa constrictor hadn't moved -- not even a hair's breadth -- since they had first caught sight of each other. *Jesus, look at that concentration*! He relaxed a few of the thousand layers of fear which enveloped him, just enough to begin sensing that the snake meant him no harm. *Yeah, I guess everybody has to live somewhere, right? I mean, I'm in your home, and actually you're being pretty decent about it. Thank God.* Bhikku Anatto wasn't quite ready to wrap the boa around his neck like a feather dancer or play flute to incite its movement like a snake charmer, but his earthquake of terror was gradually subsiding into a series of aftershocks.

The two figures sat motionless for nearly three hours until the sun rose, at which time Shiva, as the giant boa had

16

by then been named in the bhikku's mind, calmly slithered back into the deep crevice which his tail had never left. Bhikku Anatto got up quickly; too quickly, it turned out, for all the excitement his body had endured, and he barely made it to the mouth of the cave before vomiting.

After cleaning himself and his robes in the stream and sweeping and freshening the dirt all around the entrance to Shiva's cave, the bhikku sat in full sunlight and reveled in the warmth of the sun and how good it felt to be safe after a night of terror. Words of the Achaan entered his thoughts. *How amazing are the countless states of mind, so compelling yet so transitory, urgent in one moment and a dream in the next.*

Boy, is that true! But transitory or not, I think I'll just let Shiva have his cave back. He glanced toward the cave and thought, *So long Shiva. Thanks for the experience. We'll have to do it again in another life.*

That's when the terrible hammer of reality dealt a crashing blow to the base of Bhikku Anatto's head. *Oh my God, where am I going to go? I can't find my way back, and the rest of the jungle is at least as dangerous as the cave!*

Mental chaos set in once again, Bhikku Anatto struggling bitterly against the only rational conclusion: He had to stay put for six more days and nights. If he tried to sleep outdoors he would be prey to bloodsucking leeches and even occasional tigers or other big cats. The only rational plan would be to sleep a few hours during the day, when it seemed that Shiva was also sleeping, deep within the walls, and then stay awake every night, all night, keeping an eye peeled for Shiva's likely return. Nervously, Bhikku Anatto stepped back inside the cave and, indeed, soon fell sound asleep.

By the fourth night of his unique retreat, Bhikku Anatto was beginning to direct his thoughts toward Shiva, who himself seemed a reptilian monk, emerging at the same time each night, sitting in the same position, in the same place, his meditative gaze fixed calmly on the human intruder in his midst. Bhikku Anatto still feared him greatly, of course, but by then the fear had gained a quality of awe and respect as well, as one might fear a great spiritual master. The bhikku even imagined that he could see compassion emanating from Shiva's eyes. After all, the great snake could obviously sense the young man's terror, so it was quite possible he could be moved to compassion for the frightened creature in his midst. Shiva was quite likely old and certainly in harmony with his life and his world. And he exuded an intelligence bordering on wisdom which eventually penetrated all but about a hundred layers of Bhikku Anatto's fear.

On the sixth night it struck Bhikku Anatto that the week was nearly over, and he was astonished to feel waves of disappointment that he would soon be parted from such a magnificent being. He looked at Shiva and, abandoning his vow of silence, spoke aloud. It was the first time a human voice had ever broken the silence of that cave.

"Shiva, I honor you. Somehow I think you know that by now. I...I'm grateful to you for something, though I'm not sure what that is. Or maybe I do know. You're perfect. You have grace and dignity and strength. You're like a Buddha."

The huge boa constrictor looked at Bhikku Anatto with such human compassion, one could almost imagine tears flowing down from his glassy round eyes.

"Shiva, I caused a terrible wreck. I destroyed the lives

of two innocent people. I..."

Bhikku Anatto suddenly broke into tears and sobbed disconsolately for several minutes. The great snake remained absolutely still.

"I... I don't know anything; I don't know what's going to happen to me. I don't know how to get past this. But somehow, you have touched my deepest soul. Just knowing you, I can't think of suicide anymore. I don't even know why, I just can't. I can't kill myself. But I don't know how to live with myself either. Oh Shiva, please wish me well, Venerable Sir. I feel blessed to have visited your home. Thank you."

Filled with gratitude toward Shiva and hope for himself, Bhikku Anatto lay down on his sleeping mat although it would be several hours before the sun rose. Entrusting his life to the great snake, he fell asleep, feeling more protected by Shiva than endangered.

When he awoke it was full daylight and Shiva was nowhere to be seen. Bhikku Anatto performed a tireless day of meditative practices, observing each step, each movement, each juicy bite of guava and mango, each breath. He felt more positive than he had in months. But when he retired to the cave for his final night, Shiva didn't appear. After a period of insecurity and disappointment, Bhikku Anatto remembered something one of his teachers had read to him, *Things and people come into our lives and then they leave us, and we are left sad and aching because of our attachment.* He realized that he had received an excellent teaching all week long, and it would be sheer idiocy to allow such a gift to devolve into sentimentality. Bhikku Anatto vanquished his neediness and smiled. He joined his hands, palms together, in front of his chest, and bowed slightly with his eyes closed. *Thank you, Shiva. Anjali. I honor the presence of God within you. Anjali.*

*

On his way to the familiar bamboo door of the achaan's kuti, Bhikku Anatto thought, *My God, it's been just one week since my last interview. It seems like a lifetime ago. I wonder whether the Achaan knows about Shiva? Was that cave a setup? Could it have been?*

And while his mind was thus occupied on thoughts other than walking, Bhikku Anatto stumbled over a banyan root and fell flat on his face. Picking himself up from the dirt, he had to appreciate the humor of such an excellent reminder that even the loftiest distractions from the present moment are yet distractions. *Thanks Buddha; I get it.*

"And how is your practice, Bhikku Anatto?" Once more, the interview thus began.

Bhikku Anatto looked into the eyes of his teacher as he had the previous week, but now the Achaan saw an entirely different young man, one who had finally begun to unlock his inner reservoirs of courage and self-honesty. Although he had seen that process of spiritual unfoldment occur, through the years, in thousands of young faces and thousands of young eyes, the sight nevertheless moved him to ecstasy in each such encounter, as though it were the first time he had ever been privileged to witness spiritual growth.

Seeing the Achaan's happiness, Bhikku Anatto understood instantly that he needn't explain about his encounter with Shiva, or inquire as to whether the giant snake was real or imagined, or even whether perhaps the Achaan himself had assumed the guise of a snake to guide

20

the young man's retreat. *Bare Reality*, Bhikku Anatto reminded himself. And bare reality was that he had indeed made significant progress along his journey of insight.

But suddenly the sadness began to emerge once again in Bhikku Anatto's heart and throat. Still looking at the Achaan, his eyes pled for help.

"Let the sadness come, Bhikku," the achaan spoke gently. "You have struggled well with fear now, so do not be afraid of your sadness any longer."

"But Venerable Sir, you teach that we must remain in the present moment," Bhikku Anatto replied as his voice began to choke up with emotion, "and my sadness clings to the past."

The Achaan said, "Bhikku, your sadness is in the present, not the past. It lives in your heart like a giant snake." Cold chills ran up Bhikku Anatto's spine when the Achaan said that. He continued, "You are afraid it will destroy you. You are afraid your sadness will wrap itself around your heart and crush you with its terrible force."

"But sadness lives in your heart simply because that is where it lives. Like the snake, sadness is not evil or chaotic, though it may be exceedingly dangerous if you ignore or battle it. It can be a powerful companion which rests unmoving, gently, within you, and strengthens your concentration and compassion."

"But Achaan, I was reckless and uncaring all my life, I never felt anything toward other people, especially strangers. I drove a car while I was drunk, and killed a... killed a woman... and her three-year-old daught...."

Bhikku Anatto finally lost control and broke down utterly, more so even than he had in the hospital three years earlier, when he first heard the tragic news. The

Achaan sat unmoving, just like Shiva, more powerful and helpful through stillness than anyone could have been through action. When he regained his voice, Bhikku Anatto continued,

"You said that awareness conquers suffering. Now you say I must live with my sadness. I can't live with it. I can't bear it. I only want to be free from the pain."

The two men sat quietly for a few minutes, and then the Achaan said, "Do you remember the story of the Buddha and the mustard seed?"

Bhikku Anatto did not respond.

"A woman approached the Buddha, carrying her dead child in her arms, and begged, 'Master, please use your powers to save my child.' The Buddha caressed the boy's corpse with tremendous compassion, but then said to the woman, 'Go back to the village, and bring me even a single mustard seed from the home of a family which has not experienced sorrow, disease, and death, and I will heal your child.' The woman returned, of course, empty-handed, and the Buddha said, 'How can I violate the nature of things? It is our task to experience fully the nature of things, not to avoid or defeat it. Peace cannot be attained either by aversion to or preference for the countless transitory phenomena, but rather by awareness of the unchanging nature in which all experiences arise and pass.'"

The Achaan saw that he had lost Bhikku Anatto by then, so he became more personal. He leaned forward and almost whispered, "You cannot conquer your sadness by destroying it, but only by accepting it and allowing it to be as it is -- unbearable sadness within an infinite nature which also contains joy and even bliss. Look into my eyes, bhikku."

The young man slowly raised his head to a level with the Achaan's.

"Do you see in my eyes an ignorance of your pain?

Bhikku Anatto did not respond, but there was no doubt that the achaan's eyes showed no ignorance at all. They were clearer than crystal, and shone brightly with unconditional compassion and understanding.

"What you see," he continued, "is that I accept your pain fully. I am not afraid to feel it. I have conquered the illusion that such terrible pain may destroy me. The pain is what it is, and I am what I am."

"You too must accept your pain fully. It will not destroy you if you share the cave of your heart with it, with respect for its power and influence on you. It will only destroy you if you ignore it or do battle with it."

The young man finally found his tongue. "But Achaan, I killed two people. I killed two people. I...," but he couldn't find any other words.

The Achaan replied, "Yes, that was a great sin. And your sadness from that act will live within the cave of your heart all your life, because that is its proper home. But that sadness is also the birth of your love and compassion for all of humanity. Some achieve Buddha nature through curiosity, some through joy, some through diligence. You will become a Boddhisattva through sadness. Let it pass through you, let it cohabit you, not only your personal sadness, but even more -- the unbearable sadness of all beings. Let all possible sadness and regret find a home within your heart, along with immeasurable compassion for yourself and all beings who experience such pain. That is what Christ did on the cross. He took on all suffering, he

23

took on the very nature of suffering itself; took it within his heart and allowed it to be just as it is."

"He did that for you in the way that you now will do it for all other beings. When villagers or other monks look into your eyes, they will see that you are one who knows their pain, who knows their sadness, who knows their shame and regret. And yet you will walk unafraid, you will live without constant distraction or aversion. You will allow joy, humor and happiness to wash over you as well. You will be all men, all women, all beings; you will hold all pain and all joy with respect and in peace. This is why we practice, bhikku. This is Buddha's Way."

Bhikku Anatto glanced over the shoulder of the Achaan and focused on a small bronze statue of Buddha sitting in meditation. All at once he finally understood why the villagers gladly share the very best of their meager food stores with the monks. He bowed respectfully to the Achaan, placing his forehead at the elderly man's feet, his heart filled with anticipation, joy, courage, fear, and sweet sadness.

THE SLOWEST WAY

THE SLOWEST WAY

Doug Swanson landed on the hard steel cot with a thud as the cell door slammed shut behind him. "Have fun for the next 60 days, asshole!," one of the officers taunted, and then continued, almost under his breath, "Son of a bitch."

But despite Doug's cuts and bruises and the laceration under his left eye which made his whole face feel like the sun, his spirits were lifted a little by the guard's anger. *At least I got to those bastards!*

Doug had made it to the top -- or bottom, depending on how you look at it. He was one mean hombre, a fuck-you convict who refused to make the state's job any easier. If it cost $23,000 a year to lock up the average con, he'd make damn sure they spent twice that much on him. "Goddamn bastards. Goddamn BASTARDS!"

He looked around his new cell. *So this is the infamous Catacombs; the joint underneath the joint; the worst place a convict can land. Well, fuck 'em where they breathe. I don't need a goddamn tv dayroom, and I don't need to listen to the 24-hour-a-day jive bullshit from other cons moaning about this and bitching about that or whacking off to their favorite songs on the radio. Fuck 'em all.*

The Catacombs: a windowless, underground vestige of historical insanity, a tunnel-of-hate ride through a punitive amusement park. For correctional officers, duty in the Catacombs was like an assignment in Siberia. For uncontrollable inmates, it was the end of the line. Built in the mid-1800's, the Catacombs was the brainchild of a lunatic architect who convinced prison authorities that criminals might be "broken" of their miscreant spirit by stripping them not only of their freedom, not only of their association with other human beings, but even of their sense of direction and their awareness of day and night. Being in the catacombs was the closest a human being might come to being nowhere at all. Guards learned the directional codes posted discreetly along the maze-like corridors, but inmates would have a hard time finding their way out even if their cell doors were left wide open.

Demented as it may sound to the modern mind, the Catacombs came out of what was then the most liberal, enlightened thinking about rehabilitation. When the Catacombs was built, Eastern State Penitentiary in Philadelphia -- the first prison in the U.S. -- was floundering after more than fifty years' effort to redeem lost souls through "the virtue of solitude", with no companion other than a Bible. Auburn Prison in Auburn New York, the second "house of penitence" in the U.S.A., didn't seem to be having any greater success through its added component of endless hard labor -- "the virtue of industry". The humane Quaker notion of spiritual redemption as an improvement over corporal punishment and public humiliation thus remained a radical and unproved idea, hence fertile grounds for experimentation. If a social scientist or architect with proper credentials were to suggest a facility where criminals would stand on one foot for eight hours at a time and stare into the sun, it probably would have been attempted.

But that was long ago. And if modern man has become no more compassionate or successful in correcting errant behavior, he has at least become less naive. In modern times, the Catacombs was not intended to redeem the handful of unruly convicts like Doug Swanson who landed there for sixty, ninety, or even the legal maximum of 180 days at a stretch; it was intended to punish them, pure and simple -- to punish, hurt, confuse, belittle, emasculate, and eventually break their contrary spirits.

*

Doug lay on his bed for quite awhile, anger slowly slipping into exhaustion. When he awoke, he didn't know whether he had slept five minutes or five hours, or even whether it was the same day. *What difference does it make, anyway? Who gives a shit? No hurry down here, no need to get on with anything else.*

He had plenty of time now. He lay still awhile, hands moving of their own accord down to his genitals, just touching for several minutes, then finally masturbating, although sweet fantasies of romance had long been replaced by disturbing feelings of rage and fleeting images of violence. Still bloody and now sticky and soiled as well, he lay still for another hour or so, slipping into deep despair.

Knowing full well that it would only make him feel even worse, Doug began to masturbate again. He was on a roll, a steady roll down to the bottom, hastening his descent by his own hand. But anger crested and released before his sexual fluids. *Wait a minute! Wait a goddamn minute here! I ain't gonna let them drive this ol' boy crazy.*

Doug the resister, Doug the outlaw, sat straight up on his bunk, his fire rekindled. After a moment, he took off his shirt, wet a sleeve with spit, and slowly began to clean himself, moistening and removing dried blood, combing his hair with his fingers, removing his pants and scrubbing them, cleaning his legs, even his feet. He resembled a cat, with a shirt instead of paws, first wetting it with his mouth, then using it to bathe himself attentively, methodically. He collected enough saliva in his mouth to gargle it around, brush his teeth with his fingers, and spit out into the center

29

of the floor into the one fetid hole which served all his "sanitary needs".

Next Doug propped his feet up on the bed and began doing power push-ups with his hands close together on the floor. As his body tired, he dipped into his reserve of rage for more strength. *50, 51, 52, goddamn bastards, 55, 56, they won't get to me, 59, 60!* He dropped to the floor panting, muscular arms pumped swollen, left eye once again throbbing with pain. After two more sets performed with strenuous determination, Doug sat Indian-style on the floor in the corner of his cell, leaning back against the wall -- a lonely, embittered human being on a cold concrete floor in the middle of nowhere -- and again fell asleep.

The crashing sounds of clanging iron doors, spit-shined boots, and jangling keys ripped into Doug's silent world like a pride of lions savaging a wildebeest. His heart raced and adrenalin surged as he tried to bring his senses to full alert. As he instinctively pressed harder into the corner of the wall and fought to remember where he was and what was going on, the clatter of footsteps stopped in front of his cell door and a gray plastic tray came sliding through a narrow slot in the bottom of the door.

Covered by shrink-wrap plastic, the tray contained one slice of white bread, cold grits, a paper cup of coffee with a paper lid, a yellowish pile of slop Doug later figured out was supposed to be oatmeal, a flattish, rectangular plastic container of water, and eight squares of toilet paper. By the end of the day he would learn that lunch and dinner were similar to breakfast, but water and toilet paper were furnished only once a day.

As much as he wanted to smash the whole tray against the door with a suitably defiant epithet, Doug had been around long enough to know there was no victory in starving himself. He ate the morning meal in about thirty seconds, slid the tray back through the slot, and gave it as hard a flick as he could to send it sliding down the polished concrete corridor, ricocheting off other cell doors along the way. *Old bad-ass Doug; you show 'em, boy.*

*

It was three or four days before it dawned on him. Doug was doing sit-ups in his "exercise room" -- he had laid out his house very precisely for his own sense of order -- when it hit him like a ton of bricks. The heating vent that he had been staring at during his workout every day. *The damn heating vent!! This place is over a hundred years old! It don't have escape-proof shit like upstairs! The goddamn heating vent! What a beautiful, sweet, motherfuckin' GORGEOUS heating vent that is! I'll show those bastards what Doug Swanson is made of. I'm gonna escape the goddamn Catacombs, whaddya think about that? I'll be a fucking legend; a convict's Houdini.*

One thing Doug knew he couldn't bear was to fail. It would be better for him to die trying. Then he'd still win, in a way. He'd go out like a man. So, it was important to do it right. The conditions were perfect for a long-term effort: Any day now, the winter heating season would be over and the furnaces shut down; he had a solid cell door so the officers couldn't see what he was doing; 24-hour-a-day dim lighting, total confinement except for ten minutes once a week when he was led to the showers, and no cell inspections. What's more, the plaster on the walls was in such bad repair he had no end of small sharp flakes to dig with, discarding them down his "hygiene hole" as they fell apart.

31

Of course, on the down side, Doug knew in his heart that any escape was always a long shot, and this one probably infinitesimal. He had no idea how long or convoluted the heating system might be, or where on the prison grounds it was vented. But it didn't really matter. He was out of choices. That dull metal heating grate held out the only fantasy of hope he could allow himself to indulge, and he had too often seen what became of men with no hope at all. He felt filled with purpose now, and that was all that mattered.

Because of his disorientation the first few days, Doug's closest accounting of his time in the hole was that he had been there between ten and thirteen days when he finally squeezed under his bunk to approach the heating grate for the first time. The heat hadn't been on in almost a week, and he wasn't sure why he had waited so long. It had certainly not left his mind for more than an hour.

Whatever the reason, he was ready now. He began the slow process of scraping away plaster, then mortar, from around the edges of the grate, catching all the scrapings in his shirt.

His first surprise came quickly: plaster dropped off effortlessly, as though it had been stuck to the wall with nothing more than spit or water. *What the hell...?* Doug's hands instinctively worked faster, and in moments the edges of the steel grate were completely exposed. It took little effort for his strong arms to work it loose from the vent shaft. What Doug had assumed would take days of struggle took only ten minutes. *Jesus Christ, somebody's done this before!*

Even though that much was clear, Doug was still stunned and a little spooked when he stuck his head in to look around and bumped his nose against a small block of wood wedged in the vent, with something carved on its surface. Moments later, his hands trembled as he twisted the scrap free. It measured about 12" by 15", almost exactly as big as the duct itself, and was in fact, Doug later deduced, a piece from the footboard of a 19th-century prison cot. Doug scrambled out from under his bed to take a good look at his curious new companion.

Only minutes earlier he had been a lone, angry convict with no thought other than escape. Suddenly, if only briefly, he was a novice in a mystery, a child unwrapping a Christmas surprise. But when Doug turned the block of wood over and looked at it in the light, his blood froze and his hair stood on end. Meticulously carved in tiny letters was the following:

chas. bishop 1896

i have escaped. you can too.

prepare yrself this is terrible passage.

strong body strong mind.

few will succeed.

slowest way is fastest.

Doug sat for over an hour, staring at the message until he wasn't even seeing it anymore. His mind wasn't prepared to deal with anything so bizarre. He felt as if his privacy had been invaded, his secret plan exposed. Yet few will succeed echoed in his mind in a way that was both frightening and comforting. Mechanically, he neatened up the area under his bed, pressed the grate back onto the heating duct, crushed and emptied the scrapings from his shirt into the hole in the floor, wrapped himself in his blanket, and passed the night sitting on his bed crosslegged with his back against the wall.

During the night, just as he was drifting off to sleep, the thought flitted across his mind, *Wait a minute -- how the hell could this Bishop dude have escaped without the hacks finding the loose grate and that board? What kind of scam is going down here?*

But hope is precious, however remote. And desperate hope can make optimists of any of us. A few hours' sleep and his morning exercise regimen drove that doubtful thought from memory.

More immediate concerns were on his mind after breakfast, when he again crawled under his bed and removed the grate. *I'm going to need some light once I squeeze inside there.* And even more importantly, *Shit! I'd need to lose 20 or 30 pounds just to get my goddamn shoulders through!*

Doug's well-muscled body had always been one of his few sources of pride, and so not an easy sacrifice to make. Sitting on his bed again holding Bishop's message, Doug thought, *This Bishop dude must have been skinnier 'n shit. Damn. Lose weight in a goddamn isolation cell... 1896...mmm...I may be the first one since then to make it. Shit, I guess I ain't got nothin to lose but the goddamn weight!*

He turned the sign over and around in his hands, then ran his fingers slowly over the weathered gray wood, through each tiny letter of every word. It was as if he now had a cell partner -- one Charles Bishop, a mysterious skinny man from another century -- and his quarters suddenly felt far less claustrophobic. *Okay, Bishop; you and me, babe. Let's do this job.*

Lunch came and Doug was halfway through scarfing it down before he caught himself. He glanced at the narrow grate, and back at the wooden message propped against his wall. *Gotta start sometime, right Bishop?* He took one more bite of his white bread baloney sandwich, savoring it as long as he could, and deposited the rest down the hole, tearing it first into tiny pieces as if his fingers could cheat out a little more taste from the parts he had given up. Over the next few days he gradually surrendered into dumping half of every meal down that awful little hole in the floor.

Whenever he felt pangs of hunger, Doug did power push-ups instead -- now fully a hundred in a set. And his dialogue with the invisible, late Mr. Bishop grew into nearly non-stop conversation, sometimes aloud, but mostly internal. *Doin' pretty well, huh Bishop? Bet I've lost ten, twelve pounds in a week.* Bishop became best friend, older brother, trusted partner in crime, but he also occasionally became a stern father figure whom Doug seemed striving unsuccessfully to satisfy. *You don't think I can do it, do you, Bishop? You don't think anybody but you can escape this hole, do you?*

And sometimes, eerily, Doug would cross the line and virtually *become* Bishop. He would hold his rectangular wooden icon for hours on end and allow it to transport him back to a time of six-guns, gallows, and a style of authority and quick justice which make our modern-day brutality seem gentle by comparison.

During those historical excursions, Doug filled in the blanks of Bishop's life -- everything other than the name "Charles Bishop" was a blank -- with extraordinary detail. Doug's Bishop stood a slight five-feet-eight and was infamous throughout the territory for his defiance to the law. He wore a handlebar moustache and was none too good-looking, but he could handle both himself and a six-gun, and took no abuse from anyone. When the law finally caught up with him, it was straight to the Catacombs and throw away the key. But Charles Bishop prevailed. He showed them all. He was the first, and possibly the last until now, to escape that miserable dungeon, and was never caught or heard from again -- or at least, that's how Doug wanted to see it.

As Doug would daydream Bishop's life, he felt Bishop's grit in his own gut, felt his pain and his pride, and most of all, his total success -- his escape to certain freedom. That vague promise of freedom buoyed him through the many hard days and nights it took to prepare himself for Bishop's terrible passage.

But as the weeks passed, neither mind nor body felt as strong as Bishop had cautioned they must be. Doug's mind was jumpy, instantly angry and mostly uncontrollable. As for his body, he had to cut back on push-ups because he simply didn't have enough nourishment to continue building muscle. *How can I get so skinny and still be strong, Bishop? What the hell's your secret; why won't you tell me, you bastard? Afraid I'm gonna make it too, and you won't be the only one anymore?*

It was in one such conversation that it happened: Doug heard a reply. Whether it was from Bishop or his own ravaged mind he would never know, but he heard it as distinctly as if he really had a cellmate. He had been lying on his bunk beginning to fondle himself -- his only remaining sense pleasure -- while simultaneously complaining to Bishop about his privations and decreasing strength. A voice from deep inside him said *Well, hell's bells, boy, it's about time to stop jerking off, start stretching out, and stop letting your mind run you ragged all day long. FEW WILL SUCCEED!*

Doug was quite accustomed by now to his unilateral conversations, but hearing a reply threw him for a loop. He quickly pulled up his pants and sat up in bed. Aloud, he cried to Bishop, "Jesus Christ, what the hell do you want from me?!" And from inside he heard, *Strong mind, strong body. Few will succeed. The slowest way is fastest.*

Without warning even to himself, Doug sprang from the bed and hurled his emaciated frame against the cell door in frustration, knocking himself to the floor. He hated it, but the damn voice was right -- in his hurry to conquer the heating duct, all he had succeeded in doing so far was starving himself. Both mind and body were weaker than when he had discovered Bishop's plaque three weeks ago. Resisting his food no longer sharpened his mental discipline; his stomach had long since shrunk and it wasn't exactly New York cheesecake he was tossing out in the first place. And as for his body -- his bones hurt, he felt old and tired, and most days found him nursing a dull headache.

Worst of all, he still wasn't able to squeeze his beefy shoulders into the heating duct for a serious exploration. He felt like a complete failure, and hated both himself and Charles Bishop equally.

*

Over the next few days Doug tried to clear his mind enough to regain his motivation. He forced himself to eat a little more -- a full supper, plus his usual half-portions of breakfast and lunch -- though concentrating more on proteins rather than wolfing down exactly half of each item. He also slowed his chewing drastically, counting fifty times for each mouthful, masticating until he swallowed nothing but liquid nourishment, easy to digest and assimilate.

His body soon felt stronger and mind was beginning to respond -- beginning to strengthen instead of atrophy. And in his escalating intimacy with Charles Bishop, Doug was now offering the remaining half of his food to Bishop as he stuffed it down the drain hole. *Here you go, pard, this Spam was flown in fresh today.*

The drain hole somehow led to Bishop, just as did the heating grate and Doug's own thoughts. Bishop was everything outside of Doug's own limitations; Bishop was freedom itself.

Doug held and stroked the little block of wood so much, it acquired a renewed smoothness from the oil in his hands. Though he knew those twenty-six words better than his own name at this point, he read them, studied them, day and night, and was constantly surprised to discover new levels of meaning to each and every line.

Stretching was very hard at first because he didn't know what to do, but as his body settled in to a series of makeshift exercises, they gradually refined themselves into a dozen barely remembered yoga postures he had learned in a federal prison class a few years earlier -- a few lifetimes earlier, it seemed.

By the end of his fourth week in the Catacombs his headaches and assorted aches and pains were gone, his mind was much clearer, and the yoga practices continued to evolve into more advanced postures in which Doug experienced fleeting feelings of well-being he had never imagined before.

Though he might have been loathe to admit it, at that point Doug was enjoying himself most of the time. His days were filled with activity. Without the slightest distraction, his energies were focused on a single goal. He learned to pace his regimen so that body and mind stopped fighting each other so much. He performed each yoga posture extremely slowly and held it for several minutes, enjoying how his mind would come almost to a standstill during those intervals -- total attention, total unity of mind and body.

Strong body, strong mind, Doug's inner Bishop would often intone. It was finally beginning to sink in. For the first time in his life, Doug was conscientiously cultivating a genuine virtue -- patience. *Slowest way is fastest, right Bishop? Bet you didn't know about yoga, you old horse-thief. Slow and steady, pardner. I'll show you a thing or two about strong body, strong mind before this escape is over.*

Feeling chilly most of the time because of his reduced body heat, and wanting to stay free of restrictive clothing for his thrice-daily yoga sessions, Doug spent day and night clad only in his blanket. He no longer shaved on his weekly shower days, letting his beard grow free. His eyes became sparkling clear from the simplicity of his diet. The lifelong angry pride on his face was gradually replaced by a mixture of humility and determination. Ironically, that desperate convict took on the look of an ancient monk, a lean ascetic quietly furthering his lonely pursuits in a small cave hidden away from the busy world above.

Yet Doug Swanson certainly didn't consider himself a monk or any form of spiritual seeker. He hadn't renounced the world; he'd been exiled from it. His ceaseless dialogue was not with God, but with a presumably dead convict named Charles Bishop. And Doug wasn't seeking a monk's enlightenment; he sought only to escape.

*

On the day of his fifth shower -- Doug's imprecise but most reliable calendar -- the officers were stunned to hear

Doug speak. "You think you fellas could get me some smokes? I've got the cash in my canteen fund."

Although those two guards had seen a number of men broken by the Catacombs, they were surprised at the degree of Doug's transformation from muscular, enraged maniac to this pathetic shell of a man entreating them for a pack of cigarettes. Neither of them uttered a response, but the next morning three packs of Camels and four books of matches, along with a crumpled commissary receipt, accompanied Doug's breakfast slop.

With a broad smile across his face, Doug -- who smoked only pot -- expertly removed and trashed the cigarettes, and gathered the aluminum foil from all three packs into an ice-cream cone shape with a small hole at the bottom. Then he patiently twisted several matches together and moistened the match stems so they would burn more slowly. Next he stuck them up into the cone, holding them erect from the bottom of the tinfoil. With another match he lit that makeshift reflector-torch and crawled under his bed to peer into the heating duct. It worked! This would do just fine to light his way through the adventurous passage waiting for him on the other side of that wall.

His first excursion into the heating duct, during what Doug estimated was his fortieth day in the Catacombs but was actually his forty-fifth, was brief and frustrating. After a short narrow section which left several cuts and scrapes along his sides, the ductwork widened a few inches and forked in three directions. Doug relit his torch and was startled to see, scratched into the duct at the intersection, slowest way is fastest.

But which way is the slowest, Bishop? Come on, man! Doug relit his torch at least a dozen times struggling to find a clue, a mark, a sign, on any of the three ducts as to which might be the slowest way . He could find no hint at all, no matter how many times he scoured the walls, trying to read something into a natural scratch in the sheet metal, or imagine a message in a random dent or seam.

Exploring just a few feet in one direction was both strenuous and frightening. *Jesus, I feel like I'm in a fucking coffin underneath the ground.* Unable to turn around, he rested for a few minutes face down on the dusty metal and then painfully backed his way out.

Resting on his bunk, he thought ahead. *I still gotta get a little looser, and I might even need some kind of grease to get through that first section without ripping myself apart every goddamn time.* In his mind he immediately saw his grandmother struggling to take off her wedding ring whenever she did the dishes, and then squeezing a drop of dish soap on her finger to make it easier. *Soap! That's what she used. But shit, Bishop, they search my ass, my mouth and ears, every goddamn inch of me after a shower. How the hell am I supposed to smuggle back a bar of soap?*

His inner dialogue responded, *Well, if you can't bring back a bar, you can leave enough soap on your body to squeeze through once a week after the shower.*

And then, optimistically, he consoled himself, *Maybe the duct system ain't that long anyway; maybe I can find the right passage my first time out.*

Later that night, Doug awoke in panic in the middle of a dream so vivid it shook him to his roots. He was naked, crawling through the ductwork, but his head was too large and forced him to keep pushing head-first to advance. He was exhausted, his head and body scraped and bruised, and either the ductwork was getting smaller or his head was

41

growing. He tried backing up, but Bishop's voice was screaming *Push!! Push harder!!*, and he seemed unable to back up even an inch. His makeshift light went out, plunging him into total darkness. The ductwork seemed to be squeezing in on him, forcing him forward even as it narrowed. Somehow a rope had become tied around his neck and was strangling him, choking him into unconsciousness. He awoke in ice-blue terror, and lay without moving for nearly an hour.

During that time, as panic subsided, it occurred to his amazement that he had relived his own painful birth. While he was a young boy he had often heard his grandmother recount the tragedy of his mother's death from heart failure just as her baby boy had crowned after fifty-three hours of labor, and how he had finally been yanked from her lifeless womb with the umbilical cord wrapped tightly around his neck, and how he didn't breathe for nearly five minutes.

But those were just words, old family stories back then. He had never really felt anything about it; nothing, that is, except a clear sense of being "bad" for causing his mother's death.

But at this moment, for the first time in his dismal, wayward life, Doug felt the pain of that innocent little creature whose entry into the world was so profoundly terrifying, and who had deeply hidden that terror for so many years. Instead of being gently placed into the warmth and security of his mother's breast, he had been thrust violently into a pandemonium of bright lights, loud voices and emotional chaos. Instead of coming into a home full of gladness and anticipation, he had been dutifully taken in by his grandmother, who was a decent woman, but not disposed to properly raise another child.

Seeing himself so clearly as an innocent, Doug burst into tears and cried his heart out. It was the first gesture of friendship he had ever extended himself, and the beginning of his second virtue -- compassion. It was the first time he had ever allowed the thought, *Maybe I wasn't born bad.*

Of course, that revelation led quickly into another, far less sympathetic, one: *If I wasn't born bad, then maybe I didn't have to fuck up my whole life like I did.* Doug's mind filled with the faces of other cons he had known, about whom it was so easy to see that they lied constantly to themselves and made every excuse in the world as to why they had never been given a fair chance in life. To him, such carping came from bullshitters and losers, not a romantic outlaw like himself.

In fact, Doug had always assumed that at least he was completely straight with himself: "Listen Jack, it ain't this and it ain't that; I'm bad because I was born that way, and it ain't my dead mama's fault nor Granny's fault or society's fault or nobody else's."

Now, all at once, he saw that he was just a self-deluded windbag like the rest, and a lifetime of embarrassment and regret fell on him like a ton of bricks. *Hey Bishop, now let me get this straight -- my mother dying ain't my fault, but my whole miserable life is?! Jesus fuckin' Christ, that's a goddamn scream. That's a real laugh riot!*

Doug spent the next few hours reviewing a loosely-strung and uncomplimentary movie of his life, trying admirably to face it all without excuses. Curiously, while he felt unforgivably stupid about nearly every choice he'd ever made, some tremendous weight seemed to be lifted from his heart. On closer examination he realized what it was: his anger was gone.

Doug was overwhelmed. Six weeks in hell had somehow yielded a lesson in patience, a revelation of compassion, and now a sudden respite from his lifelong shadow of unspecified fury. *My God, I feel like a goddamn war is over. I like this. Jesus Christ, I like this a lot! Bishop, did you know about all this? Is this what you meant by "prepare yourself?" Jesus Christ, Bishop, I like this! I really like this!*

A smile beaming from ear to ear, Doug stroked his wooden touchstone for a while, then affectionately propped it against the wall at the head of his bunk. It was clearly a champagne night, a night to celebrate with friends, and Doug didn't quite know how to spend such a night alone in the bowels of the Catacombs. Without a second's thought, he stood up and began singing, "I got sunshine, doo-**doo** doo doo doo-**doo**, on a cloudy day, doo-**doo** doo doo doo-**doo**. When it's cold outside, I've got the month of May, doo-**doo** doo doo doo-**doo**. I guess, **boom**, you'll say, **boom**, what can make me feel this way --- my girl...," and by the time he had completed that first verse, Doug was sliding gracefully across the floor with perfect moves.

He continued singing and dancing through fifteen or twenty songs, non-stop, before collapsing in laughter on his bed.

I'm all right, he told himself. *I blew about thirty-two years, but I never killed nobody, I'm healthy, I've got guts, and I've even got pretty good luck, for a self-destructive asshole. I can start over. I _am_ gonna start over. Life could be a lot worse.*

Another part of his mind -- though certainly not his alter-ego Bishop -- countered, *Yeah, like how? Getting hit by a train? Look around, stupid.*

Slightly angry at that interruption of his high, he retorted, *Get fucked, all right?* Then, noticing the irony of that last exchange, Doug burst out laughing again. *Hey, Bishop, did you hear that? I just told myself to get fucked, and I deserved it, too! Ha ha ha!*

In an orgy of self honesty and humor -- two other virtues markedly absent from his entire life -- Doug continued to have unbridled fun for the rest of that night.

*

During his next shower, Doug soaped his upper body heavily without rinsing the soap off. One of the officers commented on that during the strip-search, but Doug looked off into the distance with a spaced-out look and the officers chalked up his behavior to seven weeks in the Catacombs.

Back in his cell, he waited patiently until after supper and then used his day's supply of water to moisten the soap enough for him to slide more easily into the duct. Hoping this might be the big day, Doug wore his trousers, socks and shoes, and tied his t-shirt around one ankle in case he should actually make it all the way off the prison grounds.

He sat at the edge of his bed, and the question crossed his mind whether his emotional rebirth should change his plans about escaping. After all, he had indeed lived a life of crime, he now accepted full responsibility for being in prison, even for being thrown in the Catacombs. *Maybe this is where I belong.*

Doug looked at the grate and at Bishop's wooden note. I have escaped. You can too. He looked at the cell door, and at the smelly drain hole in the center of that squalid little floor. He looked into his newfound conscience -- for with compassion, even for oneself, some degree of conscience inevitably follows.

Doug didn't have much experience with personal morality, so he sat there puzzling for awhile. Finally, he thought, *Nah, nobody belongs in here,* and chuckled. *Jesus, this "new me" stuff could get out of hand if I don't watch out!* Doug picked up his homemade torch, stuffed the remaining matches in his pants pocket, and bid his unique monastery goodbye.

*

The going was slow, and Doug fought occasional lapses into that pool of fear he had identified as birth trauma. He knew he had to limit his use of the torch, so most of his ordeal was spent in pitch blackness, feeling his way along. Bishop certainly knew what he was talking about: strong body, strong mind were needed in equal amounts for this terrible passage.

Doug spent what he guessed was about two hours inching his way down the first of the three forks in the ductwork. The passage was routine except one time in the dark when he involuntarily shrieked after placing his hand directly onto the dried, decades-old corpse of a large rat. He hated rats, whether they were running around his cell or dead for a hundred years. He lay still for a few minutes, catching his breath and hoping that no one heard him.

A little further along, his brief excitement at seeing a source of light turned to terrible disappointment when he arrived at a dead end, except for the narrow alley which led to the grate in an adjacent cell. The main duct ended right there, no further choices at all. If he hadn't been so tired and preoccupied, Doug might have noticed with curiosity that something resembling a block of wood was wedged into that narrow vent, just short of the cell wall. But he didn't look very closely in that direction.

He did, however, light up to check for any messages which might be scratched into the duct wall. Sure enough, staring at him, mocking him once again, was slowest way is fastest. *Jesus Christ!* He let his torch burn out and just lay for a few minutes face down, trying to figure out whether he could possibly turn himself around to crawl back. He finally decided he couldn't do that without breaking into that other cell and then reentering the shaft -- an option which presented far too many unknowns.

Though he was exhausted by the time he returned to his starting point, Doug was more determined than ever to be gone before breakfast. This bizarre game with Bishop was driving him relentlessly now. Pausing at the main intersection only long enough to replenish his torch with new matches, Doug backed into his own alleyway and then started forward on the second of the three passages.

When he arrived at his second dead-end, identical to the first, once again he confronted slowest way is fastest scratched into the duct wall. And he did notice this time that there seemed to be a block of wood wedged in that narrowest part of the vent close to the cell. But the lighting was so bad, his eyes so irritated by dust, and mind so scrambled from a total of nearly seven hours crawling like a mole beneath the earth, Doug was in no condition to care about the scenery. Wearily, with intense back and neck pains and nearly in tears, he began the tortuous journey backward to his starting point.

Only one direction left. *Well, that's kinda par for me, I guess; go for the two duds first!* Of course, the sober thought had flitted across his mind that the third channel

47

may lead only to an unnegotiable furnace, but such a thought held not the slightest purpose since Doug knew he had to try anyway. His chief worry was that he had lost track of time. Although he was pretty sure he hadn't used all thirteen hours between supper and breakfast, he had no idea how much time might be left. If his food tray weren't slid back within an hour from breakfast time, his plans could be in serious trouble.

Doug started off in the final direction, all along the way hoping for tremendous luck. *Maybe it's not as long as the others; maybe it forks off to an outside vent; maybe the furnace room is outside the main walls.* Unfortunately only one of his maybe's -- the least of them -- came true. In a mere half hour, Doug arrived at the hopeless end of his escape attempt.

The connection between ductwork and furnace was impassable. This wasn't a huge furnace as he had imagined, with miles of confusing but hopeful ductwork. Because of the architecture of the Catacombs, several small furnaces had to be used, serving only six cells apiece. The ducts were welded solidly onto its sides, and the only outside vent rose straight over the firechamber like the stovepipe from an old woodstove.

Doug was devastated. He cried from disappointment, pain, and exhaustion. Soon, his concern about time came back into his mind and with great difficulty he forced himself to inch steadily backward to his cell. He hadn't bothered to look for clues -- or rather, sadistic taunts -- at the end of his passage, because he knew with certainty what he would find, and couldn't bear to see it again.

Along the way, his anger returned full force, and every ounce of it was directed toward Charles Bishop. *You goddamn sadist motherfucker, you... you...* but no words could express the degree of loathing which consumed Doug's mind. At one point the image of a small wooden block wedged into that adjacent cell's vent returned to his mind like a tornado. *Jesus Christ! That goddamn thing's in every cell, isn't it? You suckered me and I fell for it! I lost thirty or forty goddamn pounds for this, you bastard! Oh God, I can't believe this!*

Doug Swanson returned to his cell a broken, beaten, bitter man and fell instantly asleep without caring to reposition the grate or neaten anything up in case his cell door were unexpectedly opened.

*

The first thing Doug did on reentering the mainstream prison population a week later was to head for the library. By then he had become obsessed with his bitterness toward Charles Bishop, as though they had been partners and Bishop had turned him in, or testified against him, or stolen his share of a score.

I've got to find out more about that no-good son of a bitch if it kills me. If only he was alive, I'd kill that fucker!

But although the prison library featured a thorough history of the institution along with an alphabetical list of inmates from the day it opened through the current year, Doug could find no mention of Charles Bishop in those lists. The only Bishops at all were teenaged twin brothers who were incarcerated from 1943 - 1961 for raping twin sisters after a church hayride. And neither of the brothers was named Charles.

Doug seethed with mystery for days. It seemed to hardly ever leave his mind. *If he wasn't a convict, then who the hell was he -- the furnace repairman? Is this just some practical joke? I'll kill somebody!*

To make matters worse, Doug couldn't talk about his secret struggle to anyone. Attempted escape added an automatic fifteen years to a prisoner's sentence, and Bishop's folly was certainly not worth an extra minute tacked on to Doug's time. For that same reason, Doug had finally restored Bishop's message to its original place and had done a crude replastering job using peelings from other parts of the wall, before he had left the Catacombs.

But in rare quiet moments in the middle of the night, when self-honesty tended to peek out from under its covers more so than in broad daylight, Doug had to admit that the entire ordeal was not without its value.

First of all, he had experienced the repressed trauma of his own birth and his mother's death, which released a lifetime of terror, guilt, abandonment and sorrow. He couldn't regret that. Then there was the acceptance of full responsibility for the mess he had made of his life. That was hard to fault also, especially since he harbored hopes now for a saner path for himself on his next release in about two more years.

Then there was the vivid recollection of sliding around his cell singing golden oldies, possibly the most fun he'd ever had. *Yeah, Bishop, you fucked me over royally, but we had our times, didn't we?*

And in the middle of the night, in the midst of those gentler reminiscences, Doug suddenly longed to hold that weathered little scrap of wood just once more. *Man, that thing... I don't know, it was really something.*

He saw himself so clearly, sitting on the bed in the Catacombs, holding and occasionally rubbing that little block of wood with such affection, as if it were his lifeline to the freedom he so desperately sought. *Yeah, I thought it was, too, you bastard. I held that thing like Granny used to sit with that old Bible of hers -- just sit for hours, not even reading it, but just holding it and rocking in her chair.*

Doug bolted straight up in his bed. *Oh my God, that's it, isn't it, you son of a bitch? And that's why you had 'em in the other vents, too! Jesus Christ, is that it, or am I fucking crazy?*

It seemed like forever for those last few hours of night to pass and the cell doors to open. Doug darted toward the library. He didn't feel the morning chill, he just felt afire with the mystery raging in his gut. At the library, he opened the book not from the back, where the lists of inmates were printed, but from the front, toward the sections describing the opening of the old territorial prison and the pioneers who became its first staff.

Well, damn, at least I was right about the moustache! There on the page, staring right back at him with a unique twinkle in his eye, was Charles Bishop, the prison's first chaplain, a man who innately understood the single flaw behind the Quaker's prison-as-penitence idea at Eastern State Penitentiary.

After staring at the photo in amazement for several minutes, Doug finally read the caption underneath: Charles Bishop, chaplain from 1872 - 1896, a true innovator in the field of corrections, whose enduring accomplishments may never be fully known. At left is an excerpt from his controversial lecture to the first annual conference of the American Penitentiary Association in Denver, 1896, after which he retired from this institution and from the field of penology.

"The comfort of God is hard enough to find for the righteous, thus how can we expect to force our own desires for spiritual release on errant men who don't want any such thing? Forcing Bibles upon our captives will not correct them. They must correct themselves through struggle and self challenge. We must give them not preachments and exhortations, but formidable opportunities to develop virtue and their God-given strength of character.

We must find and speak a common language with our charges. The foremost desire in a prisoner's mind is to escape. In actual fact, a prisoner's desire to escape should not be suppressed by us, but discussed and explored, and ultimately redirected within himself. We must encourage him to see that escape from the institution is fraught with peril and quickly ended, while escape from one's own vices and delusions leads to spiritual freedom.

I know many of you find my views naive, as I do yours. In all fairness, we must acknowledge one to the other that so far as criminal redemption is concerned, few will succeed either way. Few will succeed. But as a humble servant of the Almighty, I must dedicate myself to the genuine, hard-won salvation of those few rather than the superficial religious coercion of the many. Perhaps this is the slowest way for us to proceed. I argue that not. But perhaps the slowest way is the fastest way in these matters, both for us as individuals and for society as a whole."

Doug's eyes darted back to the caption, whose enduring accomplishments may never be fully known , and at once he saw vivid scenes of himself in the Catacombs, discovering his real strengths and weaknesses, devoting himself so patiently toward a single goal, unmasking his compassion and playfulness, his resourcefulness and perseverance. Charles Bishop was still the active chaplain in the Catacombs, even in the 20th century!

Once again, just as in the Catacombs, Doug felt an oppressive weight lifted from his breast. Forgiveness, combined with gratitude, had sneaked into his mounting collection of virtues. He felt good again -- very good. Charles Bishop had left behind a curious little wooden Bible for just "a few" desperate criminals to discover, and Doug had been lucky indeed. If he had merely escaped the prison as he had hoped, by now he would probably be on his way back inside, or possibly dead.

Instead, an old, rascally maverick of a preacher had tricked him into escaping his own anger, fear, dishonesty and pride. It was a dirty trick, for sure, but then, Doug would never have fallen for a clean one. Now he had a strong body and strong mind, and the patience to take a slow way. He had a couple of years to "prepare" himself, and he intended to do just that.

After several hours of affectionate revelation gazing at the photo of Charles Bishop and rereading his words again and again, Doug raised himself slowly to a standing position. In the unseen sky far overhead, the sun approached its noontime position where it seems to shine equally in every direction. Below, in the muted light of the prison library, a solitary figure shut the covers of a dusty old book and began to move rhythmically toward the door.

*I've got sunshine, doo-**doo** doo doo doo-**doo**, on a cloudy day, doo-**doo** doo doo doo-**doo**....*

A MATTER OF CHOICE

A MATTER OF CHOICE

Every head in the congregation was nodding now, slowly, soberly, hanging on every word Reverend Bumgardner spoke as if each syllable were uniquely, intimately addressed to each of three hundred different hearts. He loved this part of his Sunday sermons. Afire with passion for God, arms rising or falling as his divinely inspired thoughts found perfect expression, Calvin Bumgardner virtually ceased to exist during those few precious moments each week. In his place stood a Divine Messenger, a classic apostle of Jesus Christ.

"When our Lord said, *I am with you always*, HE DID NOT MEAN merely through the pages of the Bible -- although the Bible is surely His inerrant Divine Word. HE DID NOT MEAN merely through the accomplishments of his twelve disciples -- although their actions did change the course of human events forever. HE DID NOT MEAN that he is with us always as a sentimental memory, like our dearly departed mothers and fathers and other loved ones -- although we cherish such memories, as well we should. And HE DID NOT MEAN that he is with us only on Sundays, in these church services, when we gather together to pray and to bless His Holy Name -- although most assuredly He is here with us, right here in Keyhole Baptist Church."

While half the heads continued to nod silently, the other half murmured a respectful "Amen" at that point, and Reverend Bumgardner paused before he went on. Even during his pause, the attention of his entire congregation, children included, remained riveted on his intense, near-ecstatic face.

"No, although any of those blessings would have been more than enough, our Lord didn't stop there." The lanky young Texan leaned abruptly toward the upturned faces of the listeners to his left.

"He didn't stop at the Bible, did he?"

About a hundred mouths quietly muttered, "No."

He looked to his right. "He didn't stop at the Apostles."

About 150 voices responded, "No." Some of the smaller children could be seen shaking their heads from side to side, as if to say "no" more solemnly than their tiny voices would allow.

Looking up at the balcony Reverend Bumgardner raised his voice, "He didn't stop at our sentimental memory of the crucifixion and resurrection -- the most perfect acts ever performed on this Earth, did he?"

Nearly every voice now, almost hypnotically, "No."

"And does He stop even at His spiritual influence through His churches which have spread to every corner of the Earth?"

The entire congregation chimed, "No."

In a quiet tone now, building with each word, with his eyes closed and his own heart nearly bursting from sheer gladness of spirit, Reverend Bumgardner breathed deeply of that feast of spiritual fervor and continued, "When Our Lord Jesus Christ, the One True Son of the Almighty God, the Alpha and Omega of all human existence, the immortal, resurrected Prince of Light and Son of Man, said *I am with you always,* He meant it literally, exactly, unceasingly, and forever -- and He meant it personally to me and you and you and you and you, and to every human being with eyes to see and ears to hear of His Glorious Love and Promise for our eternal salvation from sin. He is HERE. He is here right now, in my heart and in your heart just as surely as we have blood in our veins and hair on our heads. He is HERE. Not poetically, not rhetorically not metaphorically; please understand me: HE IS HERE. PRAISE GOD!"

On that final word, his hand slammed down on the oak pulpit with a thundering sound that seemed to hang in the air as the congregation sat stunned in silent amazement. The entire church felt awash in Holy Spirit. Three representatives of the Evangelical Broadcasters Network who sat in the first row had by then forgotten entirely that their presence in Keyhole, Texas, was more business than worship. For the moment, they were swept utterly off their feet. Handsome, tanned, radiating health and sincerity, raised in a small town and married to his high-school sweetheart, Calvin Bumgardner was the broadcasters' find of the century. He spoke without notes, having only a general topic in his mind and trusting the Lord to help him find his words each week on the spot. He was neither a phony nor a windbag, and he loved preaching nearly as much as he loved God.

When the service ended, the EBN contingency waited patiently as Reverend Bumgardner shook hands with and fielded exuberant praise from nearly all the members of his congregation. The EBN emissaries approached him then like three wise men, brimming with certainty and confidence in the good news they had brought from afar.

"Reverend Bumgardner," Wilson Pike began as the four men sat down in the young pastor's office, "I'm going to come right to the point. We believe you have a higher calling than to tend your flock of three hundred here in Keyhole. We would like to offer you the opportunity to shepherd a flock of more than three *million* -- maybe *thirty* million before long. You have a gift, son, and it is our privilege to invite you to make the best use of that gift for our Lord's sake."

Calvin didn't know what to say. Bud Harrod, another of the three, added, "You wouldn't even have to leave your present congregation. We will build you a new church right here on this spot or anywhere else you want, to hold seven thousand people, and to accomodate our satellite equipment so that you'll hardly notice any fuss at all while you're preaching."

Seeing that Calvin was not close to response, Harrod added, in a measured, quieter tone, "We're talking about saving souls for the Lord, Reverend Bumgardner. Saving millions of souls, witnessing your extraordinary faith to hundreds of countries across the globe, and accepting God's own gifts of esteem and financial prosperity in return. Your initial contract with EBN would include a new parsonage, $125,000 a year salary, comprehensive insurance and travel expenses for you and your family, and a seat on our Planning Council for Domestic and Overseas Evangelical Projects. You can do good works in this world to a degree beyond your wildest imagining, Praise God!"

After a full minute of silence, the third and eldest visitor, the Reverend Caleph Haas, said softly, "Gentlemen, we've given this fine young man quite a bit to think about. Why don't we let him pray upon it and call on him again tomorrow?"

Calvin Bumgardner raised his head slightly and said, "Yes, I... I'd, uh, I'd like to do that, yes," seeming an entirely different person from the confident, passionate preacher they had heard from the pulpit only forty minutes earlier.

*

60

The sound of the phone jerked Calvin's head up from his desk and set his heart racing. His office was dim now, the late afternoon light filtering through a hundred-year-old black oak outside his east window. The phone rang three times before he had regained his senses enough to answer.

"Shug, what's wrong?," Darlene's honeyed drawl inquired. "Why aren't you home yet? I've got supper on the table and the Farrises are here; we're all waiting on you, hon."

Still groggy, Cal said, "I'm awful sorry, I had some thinking to do, and I guess I fell plumb asleep sitting here at my desk. What time is it getting to be?"

Darlene replied, "It's 5:30. You told me you'd be home by three o'clock. What was it you were thinking about? Well, actually, never you mind that right now; you can tell me later. Just come home right this minute, all right?"

"Yeah, I'll get myself together here and be home in a half-hour. Tell the Farrises I'm sorry."

"Okay shug, I'll see you in a little bit."

Sitting motionless with his hand still on the phone for a minute or two, Cal finally yawned a great big noisy yawn, stretched his arms up as far as they could go, and rose from his desk. He was halfway across the room before he saw his visitor.

Sitting inconspicuously in the shadows on the leather sofa opposite Cal's big east window was a man.

"What the...Who...what do you want?" Cal tried to conceal his fear as he spoke. He firmly believed that true faith conquered all fear, and he never liked being reminded that his faith was less than perfect.

"Don't be afraid," the man replied, steadily. "I just want to talk with you, Reverend Bumgardner."

Questions raced through Calvin's mind: *How did he get in? How long had he been sitting there, watching me sleep? Was he an escaped convict from the Waco prison unit down the road?*

Regaining his professional composure, Cal said, "I'm sorry, friend, but I'm on my way..."

The quiet intruder interrupted, "home to your barbecue supper with the Farrises, I know. But I do need to talk with you, Reverend. Please."

Cal stepped closer to the sofa now. The man seemed to be in his early thirties, of medium height and build. He was clean-shaven, though his dark brown hair looked unkempt, and he wore faded blue jeans and a light blue t-shirt. His eyes remained in the shadows, but Cal could see from the set of his face that this was a man of sensitivity and intelligence. And his voice -- well, there was something strange about that voice. It was at once entirely new, yet completely familiar.

Cal pulled a chair over from his desk and sat down. "What is this all about, friend?"

"It's all about you, Reverend Bumgardner. It's about you and the choice you're about to make. It's about serving two masters poorly or one perfectly."

"What do you know about it, and who *are* you, sir?"

The visitor slowly straightened up and leaned forward toward Cal, bringing his face full out of the shadows. He looked directly into Cal's eyes and a convulsive wave of fear rippled visibly through Cal's entire body. Cal looked straight down at the floor, unable to maintain eye contact.

His heart raced nearly as fast as his mind. *Could I still be asleep?* He looked closely at the floor, at the details of his shoes and pant cuffs.

"No, this isn't a dream, Cal," the visitor patiently spoke, as if he could read Cal's mind. I am He. I am with you always, right here, just as you preached so eloquently this morning. Sometimes I appear in one form or another; for example, around two years ago when I spoke with old Mrs. Oliver in her garden. Remember, she told you all about it, and you gave her a nice pat on the head and congratulated her, but you didn't believe her at all. You didn't believe I would do that. And now you find it impossible to believe this, even while it's happening. Faith is a funny thing, isn't it?"

The moment he stopped speaking, the man leaned forward a little further and touched Cal's shoulder softly, just the slightest tap. Cal felt his heart swell to bursting, and broke down crying as he had never cried before, like a wanderer who had found his home after forgetting that he ever had one. He cried and cried, and his tears seemed to carry away his confusion, fear and conflict as they ran down his face. He did indeed love God! My God, how he loved God!

Cal didn't know how long he had cried, but now it was subsiding, and he raised his head toward the man, stopping just short of direct eye contact.

"Lord, forgive me. Forgive me my lack of faith, and forgive me my sins. Forgive me for being unworthy of you. Forgive me..."

The visitor cut in good-naturedly, "How about a blanket forgiveness? I forgive all your shortcomings, real and imagined. Now, we need to talk."

63

Everything in the stranger's manner was ordinary and patient. He spoke softly with a hint of humor, sometimes irony, in his voice. This wasn't at all as Cal would have expected a Divine Appearance. But the reality of His eyes, the rarity of the atmosphere charging Cal's office like an oxygen chamber, the magical glow brightening the room enough not to need the lamps, and of course the profound feelings in his heart, more than overcame such expectations.

The visitor continued, "The three men from Evangelical Broadcasting Network made you quite an offer. What does your heart tell you about it?"

Cal found his voice, cleared it, and replied, "I don't know, Lord. What should I do? Anything you want me to do, I'll do it; I swear."

"What does your *heart* tell you about it?"

"I don't know, Lord! I'm so confused!"

"Not the mind, Cal; the heart. Listen closely."

The visitor closed his eyes and concentrated, so Cal did the same. He turned his attention inward, and suddenly all noise of mind ceased for the first time in his life. His brain was quiet, his sense of self momentarily released from its prison in the skull. Now he found his awareness moving downward, to the center of his chest, and he discovered a presence, and thoughts, feelings, and conscience so clear it astounded him he was unaware of them a moment earlier.

Resoundingly obvious in that heart-place was the realization that he had always been turned off to EBN and the other opulent high-tech ministries which seemed to battle each other for ratings more than turning souls to the humility of the Christ. But his mind had repressed such feelings out of fear of being judgemental, and out of a sincere desire to avoid conflict within his denomination.

While he sat in this place of the heart, marvelling at his unprecedented self-honesty and stillness of mind, Cal found his head lifting, eyes opening, and found himself looking directly into the eyes of that God-man before him.

But now the visitor's eyes weren't at all as Cal had perceived in his first glance. They weren't frightening to Cal's heart as they had been to his mind. Now they seemed to be simple eyes, childlike, open and free. They were happy eyes, unburdened of any and every fear in the mind of man.

The visitor smiled and said, "Now *that's* your heart, Reverend. And in your heart you know all manner of things.

Cal was speechless. The two men sat staring into each other's eyes for a long while, like the clear moon and its perfect reflection. Finally, Cal found himself confessing, "Lord, I love the ministry and I love especially to preach, but now I see that I don't know what I'm talking about. I don't know what Christianity is about. Being with you right here and now is the only real thing that's ever happened to me. Show me the way, Lord. Show me my way and my calling."

The visitor smiled a happy, friendly smile, and said, "I'm so glad you asked that, Reverend. You would be surprised how many people -- especially ministers -- don't really want to see." An even stronger atmosphere now permeated the room, seeming to fill it with golden light. Cal no longer felt his own body at all. The office fell away. Texas fell away. Time itself fell away. And as Cal continued to look in His eyes, the man's face began changing.

Cal sat transfixed for quite a while, witnessing impossible changes of shape, of color, of age and race in the visitor's face. He saw men and women of every land and every era. He saw the Buddha, he saw Moses and Mohammed, Rama and Krishna, Apache and Toltec medicine men, Eskimo seers, he saw Mother Mary's angelic face change into the bloody, terrifying visage of the Hindu Goddess Ma Kali, destroyer of ego and impurities, and then again into Durga, the gentle Golden Goddess. Cal saw thousands of faces and forms emerge before his astonished eyes, whole civilizations rising and falling, wars and births and deaths, massive herds of buffalo thundering across the prairie, baby birds emerging from the tiniest eggs, beggars and street waifs, kings and queens, world leaders and nameless factory workers, and finally the visitor's face resumed the look which fit so naturally and inconspicuously on that body in those jeans in the state of Texas, planet Earth, 1988.

The visitor rose to His feet as Cal's whole body quietly shook with awe and mystery. He put his hand directly on Cal's heart, and Cal closed his eyes as he continued to shake.

Cal's mind became quiet once again. And again, the sudden clarity of his insights and feelings astounded him. He saw now that the encounter had gone much further than the simple decision to join or not join the Evangelical Broadcasting Network. His entire perception of religion had been destroyed and reborn. Now it seemed absurd to differentiate between the color, likeness, nationality, or historical story of the Holy Spirit taking form among men. All that mattered was to inspire people to have faith, to turn inward to their hearts, where the one God truly dwells. Cal no longer cared at all whether people attended a church or studied the Bible or baptised their children; he saw those as nothing more than petty details, mere matters of choice of an almost recreational nature. He wanted to look into the eyes of every person in the world and say, *Just love God, and see His form in everyone and everything. Love one another and have joy, for He is in our hearts.*

As he continued to sit in silent meditation, it dawned on him that religions are like different colleges, and he had now graduated into spiritual adulthood. Could he continue being a Baptist minister, now that he had seen the universal face of truth -- now that he could no longer preach the supremacy or uniqueness of Christianity over all other religions? What would the Southern Baptist Convention say? Would even the Keyhole Baptist congregation trust his revelations if he were to describe this experience honestly? Would his own wife and children stand by him through possible exile and humiliation?

Cal Bumgardner had spent a lifetime embodying the epitome of social acceptance and religious obedience, a lifetime of being liked and likeable, of being decorous and acquiescent. He had often preached of the need for Christian courage to face personal crises, but those were crises of this world, like alcoholism or adulterous temptation or the appeal of other religions! How could he be expected to find courage so limitless that he could throw away a perfect, righteous life to be branded a deluded troublemaker? How could a merciful God bestow such an impossible enlightenment as this upon him? An enlightenment to destroy his good name rather than distinguish it?

Filled with frustration and confusion but feeling the comfort of his Master's hand still upon his heart, Cal opened his eyes and began to plead for greater understanding, but to his astonishment the visitor was gone. Cal's head snapped down toward his chest, toward the absolutely real sensation of the Lord's hand upon his heart. All confusion

67

was suspended as he realized, *Oh my God, the feeling is inside my heart! Please don't ever leave me, my Lord.*

In his heart, Cal could hear as clear as a bell, in that ecstatically familiar voice, *I am with you always. Always.*

*

Cal looked around. His office looked and felt entirely normal, save for the shadow of one fast-moving cloud gliding silently across the floor.

Mechanically, Cal rose and got ready to go home. He glanced at his watch and saw that it was 5:32 PM, just two minutes from the time, lifetimes ago it seemed, that he had hung up the phone from his conversation with Darlene; just seconds from the time he rose from his desk to leave. But he was barely surprised. He had witnessed greater mysteries that day.

As he walked through the echoing corridors of the church, Cal's mind stepped through all of religious history -- but a different side of religious history than he had ever taught in Sunday school. Now he grasped not the endless ritualistic obedience and conformity of the masses, but the lonely trials of the mystical few in every age. In a new light he saw Christ mocked and scorned, not only by the Romans and Pharisees, but also by many of the people who had admired or listened to Him only days earlier. He thought of faces in his own congregation, the admirers who held his hand so reverently on their way out of church, and he could clearly imagine their expressions contorting into anger and fear in reaction to his revelations. He walked in the steps of countless early Christians shunned by their families, exiled, imprisoned, tortured, dying as heretics or lunatics. He saw the paths of martyrs and saints of every faith -- ordinary people like himself who felt compelled to share their visions and testimony of the One Living Spirit. He had never before conceived of those people as ordinary. He had never conceived of their humiliation or ostracism as possible in the modern world. The established societies of olden times were rife with evil and cruelty and ignorance, they couldn't have been as decent as his contemporary world of friends, congregants, and church elders! Surely in this day and age, genuine Christian experience wouldn't be seen as heresy!

Yet in his heart, there wasn't the slightest doubt that his revelations would indeed brand him demented at least, and probably blasphemous as well. All the piety and comfort and security he had spent a lifetime building would vanish in a matter of days from now. His wife would be avoided in the supermarket, his children shunned and taunted at school -- if he still had a wife and children at all. All those years that he had preached rote Biblical passages without understanding, without even considering their actuality! Passages such as *And he that loseth his life for my sake shall find it*, or *And ye shall be hated of all men for my name's sake,* now recurred to him with terrifying immediacy.

But *I am with you always* echoed now in his heart, never further away than a moment of quiet reflection. And Cal discovered he had been right all his life about true faith conquering fear, because now he watched that battle fought and won every few seconds as he contemplated the changes to come. He did indeed love God, and also God's son, with every fiber of his being. And now that he had seen His true faces -- an infinite number of them -- with his own eyes, he had grown up spiritually all at once, in an endless moment beyond time, place, or argument. It seemed amazing to him that for all his Bible study, it had never once dawned on him that humiliation, ridicule, and social crucifixion might ever arise as his own road to salvation.

Cal left the doors to the Keyhole Baptist Church wide open that night, as he left behind a respectable and rewarding life of religion in order to follow the Christ.

LINEAGE

Courage, Truth and Kindness

have been revealed to me.

Now Love, with perfect madness,

comes to set me Free.

LINEAGE

"A world of beauty and a world of despair," Shabazz said quietly, almost to himself, as he gazed out the barred window to his left.

Hector pulled himself up from one of the countless stupors he had become accustomed to during the past six weeks. "What'd you say, man?"

Shabazz repeated, "A world of beauty and a world of despair. That's what Allah must be thinking this morning as he watches this old prison bus roll along through all His beautiful creation. I mean, this tiny metal bucket full of misery, and just look out there, brother." Shabazz gazed again at the magnificence of the Shenandoah Valley, but Hector dropped his head to his chest without looking.

Six weeks on the road in handcuffs, waist chains and leg irons had been a nightmare, had made Hector Vincantos nearly numb inside and out. Herded on and off the bus like cattle, stared at in every truckstop like freaks, unchained each night on cold cement floors of one county lockup after another like rabid dogs, Hector and 29,000 other new federal convicts annually learn the worst of what "the life" is all about riding urine-stenched carriages of despair along thousands of miles of highway, long before they ever set foot inside their prison cells.

As Shabazz finished speaking, an angry voice from the front of the bus boomed, "Shut the fuck up back there!" Hector didn't look up, but from head to toe rippled a brief wave of disgust for the creature behind that voice. Justice. Incredible. If ever Hector wanted proof that there was no Allah, no God at all, officer Marion Justice's name alone would do the trick. But Hector needed no such proof. He had long ago given up on both God and justice of any sort, like most of the men around him. And though he secretly was impressed by Shabazz's sense of dignity and self-respect, that Allah stuff had made Hector too uncomfortable to become very friendly with him during this bus time.

About seven hours later, travelling due north, the prison bus finally rolled to a stop. Both bus officers stepped out to talk with the guard at the gate. Hector sleepily opened one eye to catch his first glimpse of the massive steel gates of United States Penitentiary-Littonburg. Everything he saw was gray -- gray gates, gray walls, gray faces on the dusty yard inside gray metal fences. The sky was a beautiful blue, but Hector didn't notice. He hadn't looked up in a long time.

"Paul, wake up," Hector whispered as he reached his shackled hands over to the shoulder of the black man sitting across the narrow aisle from him. "It's Littonburg, man; we're finally here."

Without opening his eyes, Paul grumbled, "You're here, man; I ain't here." Hector laughed with uncomfortable exaggeration, as he usually did when he didn't get the joke. With eyes still closed, his voice just barely patient, Paul continued, "I'm doin' bus time, man, I thought you knew that. Me, Cody, Shabazz and Williams, they got us riding the circuit -- we don't get off at Littonburg or nowhere else."

Hector had done three bits before, but this was his first time in the federal system. He was small time, not really what he had always thought of as a federal outlaw; he just crossed the state line into Oklahoma while drunk and on the lam after robbing a convenience store in Amarillo. In fact, before the reading of his charges, he had never heard of

"Interstate Flight to Avoid Prosecution." And he surely didn't know anything about this business of "riding the circuit."

In a lifeless monotone, Paul explained that he and the other three cons had been officially in transit for more than two years. Paul's big mistake was filing a lawsuit to get himself transferred closer to his family. Shabazz had forced the prison to allot chapel space more often for Muslim prayer meetings -- which they did, and then immediately moved him out to have the last laugh. Cody and Williams were merely less-than-genius characters who had badmouthed vindictive administrators on the wrong day.

Hector was stunned into silence by this new wrinkle in the endless game of mutual cruelty which cons and cops seem to play with equal dedication. Shabazz joined in and said, "Welcome to Amerika's gulag, brother Hector."

Shabazz's voice was softer than Paul's, not at all impatient. He spoke respectfully, almost formally, belying his ghetto background and eighth grade education. And what struck Hector -- and sometimes bothered him -- most was that Shabazz had no oppression in his voice. He didn't sound like a prisoner. He spoke more like a soldier, captured behind enemy lines, who is confident his army will win the war.

The three cons paid no attention to Justice as he reboarded the bus and began shuffling through papers on his clipboard. Like a political science tutor, Shabazz continued, "You see, Amerika's Siberia is on wheels, brother. This is how they get rid of you when you make waves. Now listen here, bus time legally cuts off all our visitation rights, all rights to counsel, all opportunities for education or job training or self improvement. It's all very neat and legal."

Paul chimed in, "Yeah, and the thing is, there's no time limit on riding the circuit. I've heard of dudes who was on the bus for five years."

Hector searched for some response, some word of consolation he might offer, but came up empty. He glanced over to Cody and Williams and saw their expressionless faces gazing straight ahead at nothing at all, and it was then he realized for the first time in six weeks of travel that he hadn't heard either of them utter a word. He glanced back at Shabazz, who had turned forward in his seat. Though they all rode the same bus, Shabazz seemed to know something about himself or where his life was going, and Hector instantly envied that.

But Hector certainly didn't envy this notion of riding the circuit. So, ugly as it was, USP-Littonburg was at least on solid ground, and Hector was relieved to finally be herded off the bus. The prison was huge. Though it wasn't really so old -- it had opened in 1932 -- it exuded a bleak timelessness as if it had been created by the Devil himself to spite the beauty and serenity of the Pocono mountains which framed it. Surely it approached satanic mockery to call such a monstrosity a "penitentiary" - a place of penitence and spiritual reflection. In truth this was a warehouse for the living dead.

As he shuffled through the big gates at 8 a.m., in a chain of losers linked by chains of steel from waist to waist, Hector's tired brown eyes expressed no indignity or bitterness, not even a natural defiance toward the men who prodded him along with the tips of their hickory billy clubs. Not once did he wonder how long he might be here, or whether he would ever leave this place. After all, where else was there to go?

*

Hector saw Monk that first day as three young ethnics gave him a welcome-to-the-cellblock tour. Monk was lying on his bed in the cell adjoining Hector's, reading a *Snoopy* cartoon book and occasionally looking around habitually as cons do.

Carlos Charlie said, "That old Anglo is harmless. For some reason they've got him tagged permanent close-custody. I don't know, maybe he dusted a hack fifty years ago, you know? Anyway, he don't do much, man; don't speak to nobody; just an old dude doing natural life."

Hector glanced at Monk. Except for the faint jagged scars criss-crossing the base of his throat, Monk was virtually nondescript, like a hundred thousand other aging hustlers and desperadoes who still live in such places long after their crimes, like their names, have been forgotten by the outside world.

Carlos Charlie continued, "And that dude coming around the corner down there, he stays four houses down from you, man. I'll tell you two things about that sucker. One is, he was born angry, bro, and the second thing is, he is absolutely the hairiest motherfucker on this planet. No shit."

Hector surveyed Teddy Anthimos from a safe angle. A thick carpet of hair around his chest and back made him look about thirty pounds heavier than his weight of 190. It seemed to run in an unbroken line up his neck, and it looked more or less arbitrary for him to decide where to begin shaving his face. His hands looked as if he had been costumed for a role as a werewolf, with coarse, curly jet-black hair tufting out from his knuckles nearly down to his nails.

"Don't stare, man," Raoul interrupted as Hector's attention got lost in a forest of hair. Anthimos seemed not to notice any of them as he stalked into his cell like a grim bear returning to his cave.

"Looks like a fun kind of guy," Hector wisecracked.

Paco, the youngest of the three Chicanos giving Hector the rundown, quipped, "Mmmmaa..mma..man, at least Ggg..gggo..god could'a put him like at the uh..uh..uh..Arctic region or something, you know? I bb..bb..bbb..bet the dude could go 40 below w..wi..without no cc..clothes."

Paco's stuttering called Hector's attention to him more closely than a few minutes earlier when Carlos Charlie had introduced himself, Paco and Raoul. Looking at him now, Hector thought *My God, he looks like a baby, this one.*

"Anyway," continued Carlos Charlie, "Teddy's doing back-to-back 25's and he don't expect to see the streets again, so he's always ready to mix it up. If we ever have to, we'll cut him up bad, but I'd rather stay out of his way. I still got a life outside in a couple years."

While Carlos Charlie was talking, Raoul and Paco had exchanged a familiar look, and then Raoul stood watch while Paco, slightly hunched over, was doing something with his hands after reaching into his underwear. Carlos Charlie glanced at them and said to Hector, "Hey, bro, let's do this j in your house, all right? It's on us -- sort of a welcoming party."

Hector looked at the joint being rolled in Paco's hand and said, "'preciate the j, but not in my house. No one comes into my house and I don't go in theirs, bro. Just an old policy of mine."

Carlos Charlie stiffened up a little at this refusal, but Paco quickly said "Sh..sh..shit, man, no big thing. Ww..ww.we'll light this lady right here."

Raoul joined in, "I could eat it a lot faster than the hacks could get here. They don't give a shit anyway, long as we buy it from them, man."

Pretty good dope for jailhouse, Hector thought, as his favorite fragrance filled first his nostrils and throat, and then his lungs. But unlike when he was younger, getting stoned now made him feel more distant from these compadres instead of closer to them. He closed his eyes and leaned against the wall as if he were really getting off, but he was actually wishing there were no ethnics at all in this new prison, and he could do his time like the lonely, embittered man he had become.

Carlos Charlie, the oldest of the three but still only in his mid-twenties, still hadn't fully warmed up from Hector's inhospitality about his cell. Now he took Hector's reverie as a further withdrawal and said, "Yo, let's let this brother settle in now. I guess he's had a long ride.... or something."

Carlos Charlie, Paco and Raoul headed off down the hall, and Hector feebly called after them with a "Yeah, thanks, bro's. Later, right?" Even stoned, he was aware that he didn't get off to the best start with his brothers, but try as he might, he couldn't drag up the energy to care.

Hector looked once again into Monk's cell, for no particular reason. Monk was moving about now. He looked to be in his sixties, although Hector knew it was hard to tell the age of a con who's been inside for many years. Monk was of medium height and build. He didn't have the vacancy in his eyes of a psycho, or the humorless mouth and jaw of a Bible-thumper. He didn't move cleverly like a schemer or exude angry pride like the younger cons.

Hector thought, *Not me, man, never. That'll never be me.* Oldtimers had always been half-invisible, half-repugnant to Hector, like the plumbing pipes overhead or the faded graffiti on nearly every wall. They were part of the landscape, part of the architecture, but not part of his life. Best to keep them off his mind.

He noticed a small sign that hung over Monk's bed, which he couldn't read from where he was standing. He was surprised at his curiosity, but chalked it up to the joint he had just smoked. For the time being, Monk was an insignificant part of the backdrop as Hector settled into the sort of joyless existence in which each day dragged on forever though the years seemed to fly.

*

The next morning, while Hector faced his first full day at Littonburg, the bus he had come in on was loading up and getting ready to leave.

Officer Marion Justice didn't enjoy bus time any more than the regular transfers or the unfortunate likes of Shabazz, Cody, Williams and Paul Turner. After all, three-to-eight-week tours of duty were pretty much a 24-hour-a-day watch, and Justice seemed to have been born angry toward convicts in the first place. On him, the mantle of "correctional officer" hung like a sick joke. He had no bent toward correcting. He seemed to be on a never-ending crusade to remind prisoners of their crimes, their punishment, their banishment, their hopelessness.

Harvey Hewlitt, the younger officer on the bus, didn't like to see prisoners mistreated. So during the past two weeks, he merely looked the other way whenever Justice fell

80

into one of his abusive tirades. Hewlitt didn't much care for Justice, though he observed the number one rule of the guards' unwritten code: back up your partner, and never let convicts' welfare come between officers.

But Hewlitt was discovering that acquiescence to wrong was not a free ride. He was beginning to pay his way nightly with insomnia. Telephone conversations with his wife were becoming clipped and tense as his sense of conspiracy and shame grew. Justice's viciousness seemed to cast a cloud in every direction over Hewlitt's life, and Hewlitt secretly hated him for that. *Just make it to Indiana and we're relieved of duty. God help me get away from this guy without anything terrible happening!*

As the seventeen transfers from Littonburg settled into their seats, Officer Justice stepped back toward Shabazz and said, "Thought you were pretty smart last night talking to the spic, huh?" Shabazz looked directly into Justice's eyes, neither intimidated nor unfriendly, and said nothing. Justice avoided his direct gaze, but continued, "Well, let me tell you something, Shitbuzz or whatever you call your heathen self. You put a lid on your 'brother this and brother that' and that commie goo-lag bullshit, because I don't want to hear it! You got that?"

Shabazz looked out the window, still silent, but with a bad feeling in the pit of his stomach, realizing from too much experience that there was no good way to handle a caveman like Marion Justice.

Turning to the whole bus population, Justice barked, "And all the rest of you, get this straight: Officer Hewlitt and I are God. You speak if we let you. You eat, shit, and sleep if we let you, and God help the son of a bitch who gets car sick on his seat. You will remain chained to your seats while this bus is in motion, and shackled to each other while getting off or boarding. Don't let the thought of escape even cross your wretched little minds, because there's nothing I would like better than to shoot you in the back and watch your body jerk and twitch in the dirt where you belong."

Justice sounded like a second-rate, corny impersonation of a drill sergeant. A couple of 'Nam vets among the cons couldn't tell whether he might be joking, until he got to the part about shooting them in the back. *This turkey's serious. Shit, man, we got thousands of miles to go with this asshole, and we're in chains. God help us.*

Finally, pointing to Shabazz, Justice concluded with, "One more thing: This nigger here is off limits. He's my special project. You will not speak to him, and you will ignore him if he speaks to you. But do keep an eye on him, because I want you to see what your life will be like if I make you my special project." And with that, he turned around toward the front of the bus with his left elbow extended just enough to glance sharply off the right side of Shabazz's head. The blow didn't hurt much, but the bad feeling in the pit of Shabazz's stomach grew stronger. He was in serious trouble, and there wasn't a thing in the world he could do about it.

Later that day, after heading southwest from Littonburg and driving halfway across Ohio en route to USP-Terre Haute, Indiana, Justice refused to unchain Shabazz to use the filthy little toilet in the rear of the bus. He had also passed him over when he was handing out box lunches. And since the guards and transferees had eaten a regular breakfast inside the Littonburg mess hall, Shabazz, Turner, Cody and Williams -- confined overnight in a temporary holding cell -- had missed that meal as well. Shabazz was getting worried now. There was no telling how far Justice might carry the abuse. Something inside Justice seemed to have discarded even the crudest moral restraints abusive officers normally observe. It was as if a terrible decision had been made in the darkest corners of his psyche, and everyone began to feel it.

Though Shabazz maintained an outward calm for the sake of the Muslim dignity he felt he represented, inwardly he was a frightened young boy in the midst of evil. He began silently praying for the strength to endure what might be coming, trying with all his discipline to remember that all experiences, even the very worst ones, arise from and return to Allah. As the hours passed, he watched Justice frequently, praying for the wisdom to see, instead of a monster in a brown uniform, that this seemingly wicked man, like everyone else, was in fact one more face of the Divine.

In his thirty-one years, Shabazz had quit a street gang, kicked a heroin habit, shed sixty pounds, educated himself, and overcome a lifetime of criminal values and the lingering despair of ghetto poverty. He had developed a tremendous amount of self-discipline and courage under difficult circumstances. But this was by far the hardest spiritual work he had ever attempted. His mind seethed with confusion, fear, anger, faith, and profound contradictions. They swirled around his ceaseless prayer like debris caught in a whirlpool.

The bus rolled on through Ohio, like a tiny cancer briefly interrupting the silence of open farmland, vast skies, and the moonlit lakes which reflected its passage into disaster.

That evening, offloading into the Wayne County Jail for the night, Justice shoved Shabazz as he was coming down the bus steps and Shabazz fell onto the back of the white convict in front of him, knocking him down and causing two other inmates in the chained procession, one black and one white, to stumble.

Shabazz hadn't eaten for more than twenty-four hours, and had needed to urinate for about nine hours. He became dizzy when he fell, and nearly lost control of his bladder. But he held on by a thread and managed to get up, and tried to help the white prisoner chained to him to his feet. But the instant he touched the white convict, Justice shouted, "**Hewlitt! Race war!**," and headed toward Shabazz with his billy club raised. Shabazz tried to lift his right arm to ward off the blow, but his wrists were chained too closely to his waist. The club thudded home first on his elbow, and the second time on his right ear. A painful, deafening high-pitched sound seemed to split the whole universe. It engaged Shabazz so fully, he didn't even see the third blow which crunched across the center of his forehead and cracked his skull open.

In a moment the sound of his burst eardrum stopped as instantaneously as it had begun, and all the pain left him. Shabazz suddenly found himself floating about ten feet above the ground, looking down on his own body lying twisted and bloody in a puddle of urine on the dirty concrete. Night was falling. Justice and Hewlitt were screaming at each other. The chained prisoners were shouting and moving about in chaos, but Shabazz heard none of it. To him, even the chaos was peaceful, and everything was happening in slow motion, or as if they were all moving through water.

Looking again at his body, he could see that it was still alive, bleeding profusely from the right ear, forehead, mouth and both nostrils. *I can see so clearly! It's beautiful, the way those streams of blood come together on the ground and flow like a small river into a crack in the concrete, nourishing that tiny ribbon of grass growing through the sidewalk. Lifeblood flowing, grass growing, all in silence.*

At once Shabazz understood everything he had ever prayed to understand, and it was all right. Centering his mind he thought, *La Illaha Llah Allah -- There is nothing other than God --* and joyfully allowed that precious, maimed body below to die.

*

It took only about a week for news of Shabazz's murder to spread throughout the prison system. Hector was smoking a joint with the guys outside the cellblock dayroom while they were continuing their rundown of who's who on the block. Skinny Freddy had just walked by, all 135 pounds of him stretched ever so tightly over his 6'1" frame. Carlos Charlie told Hector about him as if he were a living legend.

"He's been here for two-and-a-half years, bro, and he ain't said a single word to nobody; I mean not a word! But dig this. My first week here, I'm in the basement of the education building with five big Anglos fixing to make me their punk, right? They had me cornered about four foot from the door, you know, and I'm trying to make up my mind whether I'd rather die or be butt-fucked, and Skinny Freddy shows up. All he did was look at me and take off his coat, real calm, and he looks for a place to hang it. Now everyone's looking at him, right? The dude turns around to the doorframe and *puts a hole in the wood* with his finger, man! Then he takes a pencil out of his pocket, and he sticks it in the hole, and hangs his coat up. When he turns back around, all five guys are gone. He looks at me and smiles, doesn't say a word, and goes out the door over to the next classroom. So I'm freaking out, right, like 'how the hell...' and I go out in the hall and look through the glass door. I'm just watching him for about ten minutes, man. Skinny Freddy is sitting in the back of the class with his eyes closed. The teacher thinks he's sleeping, right, and he throws this eraser right at Freddy's head. You should'a seen it, man. Quick as a flash, Skinny Freddy catches the eraser without even opening his eyes, and then he just looks at the teacher and smiles that same smile. So now, everybody in the class is going 'ooh' and 'aahhh', you know, and word spreads and since then everybody -- even the man -- stays out of his way. And in two and a half years, nobody's ever seen Skinny Freddy get mad, get mail, or get a visit. He's weird, bro, but he's one righteous dude."

Hector watched Skinny Freddy glide silently along. As he overtook Monk going the same way, both of them stopped for the briefest moment, smiled at each other, and bowed their heads slightly like the Japanese do. Hector found that very puzzling, and watched them continue silently together down the hall until they turned a corner and were out of sight.

A moment later Carlos Charlie was pointing out Brother Malcolm, a perfectly dressed, pressed, 6'2", 208-pound human muscle who looked as though an ounce of fat had never been within ten feet of his body. His head was shaved bald daily, and his skin the deepest black Hector had ever seen.

"Man," Carlos Charlie reported, "this dude irons his t-shirts, his socks; I mean, he has got some kinda positive attitude, bro."

Brother Malcolm was a Black Muslim, which made Hector think of Shabazz. Hector noticed that Brother Malcolm wore a black armband on his sleeve.

Carlos Charlie said, "Yeah, the armband you know, it's completely against the reg's, but the man ain't gonna fuck with these Muslim dudes right now. Didn't you hear about that brother on the bus who got his head bashed in last week? Shit, man, he was probably on the same bus you came in on. He had one of those Arabian names, you know, like Shazam or something..."

Hector's gut tightened in anger. "Shabazz?"

"Yeah, that's the dude! You know him?"

As Carlos Charlie related what he had heard about Justice and Shabazz, it hit Hector hard, though he kept to himself about it. Shabazz had strength and dignity; he had held out a flicker of hope for Hector.

Hector grumbled, "I'd shove a broom up that pig's motherfuckerin' ass and break it in two."

Raoul cut in, "They've busted him, you know -- 'violating the civil rights' of Shazam by fucking splitting his head open! Man, don't you just love these dudes? I love their language, man! 'Violating his civil rights.' Shit, they'll probably stall around for a few months and turn him loose."

Paco said, "Wwww..ww.ww.well shit, man, can you imagine if they gave the pp..pp..pig time? I mm..mm.mean, where could they pp..pput him?"

"Wipsack," replied Carlos Charlie in an authoritative tone, trying as always to keep the lead. Paco looked at him quizzically. Carlos Charlie continued, "If he *does* do time, they'll put him in 'wipsack'. It means 'witness protection' or some shit like that, but they also use it for dudes like Justice because they're too hot for p.c."

Hector was no longer listening. His face seemed to darken even in broad daylight; his heart had turned to stone. The cold hatred he felt in that moment hadn't changed over millions of years of human evolution. He muttered, almost to himself, "I know that sucker's face. I don't care what name they call him. He's dead meat if I ever see him again."

Carlos Charlie started to say something, but suddenly a hideous scream erupted from the dayroom. Grifter, a tattoo freak and sometime-friend of Teddy Anthimos, ran out the door while the screaming continued. Hector and his friends stepped inside to find Teddy writhing on the floor and clawing at his eyes.

"Jeezis, man, what happened? What happened?," Raoul was yelling at Teddy, but Teddy just kept screaming and rolling from side to side on the linoleum floor.

"Oh God, man, look at that shit," said Carlos Charlie, pointing to an overturned paper cup next to a bottle of mimeograph fluid. Charlie picked up the cup and sniffed it, continuing, "Goddamn, they made hooch out of the copier shit! Grifter's a clerk in the chaplain's office, and he's always sniffing around that old mimeo machine. That stuff can kill you, man!"

Paco had never seen anyone in that kind of pain. He reached down and touched Teddy's shoulder with genuine compassion and said, "Listen, man, wh..ww..what can we..." but before he could finish his sentence Anthimos turned all his pain, fear and fury in Paco's direction and tackled him waist-high, sending them both crashing through the plate-glass window leading to the hall. Anthimos' screams hadn't paused for a moment, but had changed from screams of agony into screams of brutal madness. Six officers were now on the scene, clubbing both Teddy and Paco and ignoring Carlos Charlie's nearly incoherent attempts to set them straight on what was happening. Like the other seasoned cons who had gathered by then, Hector watched impassively while Raoul and Carlos Charlie argued with the guards who finally dragged Teddy and Paco, both semiconscious, off to isolation cells. It was four hours before Teddy Anthimos was taken to the infirmary, and by that time he was permanently blind. Paco was released from administrative segregation the next morning.

One beautiful spring day a few weeks later, Hector stood alone on the yard about thirty or forty feet from the weight benches where the ethnics were working out. How young they all looked. Though he still didn't know their exact ages, he guessed that Paco couldn't have been older than nineteen.

"Hey Raoul," said Paco, "You're getting short to the bb..bb.board, aren't you?"

Raoul finished his set of benchpress and replied, "Two weeks, man."

"You come up with a pp.pp.parole plan yet?", Paco continued.

"Yeah man, I got a BIG plan," Raoul went on, and he broke into a broad grin as he rubbed his crotch with both hands in exaggerated motions. "And you better keep your sisters inside the house, bro."

They all laughed. Carlos Charlie chimed in, "No, no, man, this is what you say to the board." Affecting mock gravity with his hands folded in front of him, he rapped rhythmically, "Your honors, I have a threefold parole plan, don't you see, which is cash, chicks, and drugs -- and making 'em all work for me." More laughter.

Hector saw himself in every one of them, young and cocky and on his way up. *When did I cross that line*, he wondered, *that turned my thoughts toward the past instead of the future?* Convict brotherhood had always been important to Hector. He wasn't by nature a loner. But at Littonburg he felt more and more out of place when he tried to hang out with the young Chicanos. And their good dope (which was no longer free to the newcomer) only seemed to deepen his depression.

Hector was grateful for their inside tips and personality profiles of Littonburg's players, but most of their conversations revolved around the streets, around their plans and desires. Hector no longer had anybody outside, he no longer allowed himself street plans and desires. His conversations were about prison stories and prison buddies. Sometimes in the middle of a story he'd think, *These guys don't give a shit,* and in all honesty, though he hated to admit it, Hector wasn't much interested even in his own stories, let alone their street jive.

Watching them now, he thought about his brothers and sister whom he had let slip from his life so long ago. He thought about how well they had all turned out, about the mystery of why he wound up a convict while they had found the mates, children, and happiness that had eluded him. *These younger guys, they probably have brothers and sisters who turned out all right, too. Why them? Why me? Were we just born bad?*

Hector leaned his head back against a wall, closed his eyes and breathed a deep sigh. *I gotta get this shit off my mind. Gotta just do the time, not let it do me.* When he opened his eyes he was startled to see Monk on the opposite side of the yard staring at him. Hector quickly looked away, but not quickly enough to avoid the train wreck in his mind.

All at once he saw the young cons, himself, Monk, and the unclaimed stiffs buried down the road in numbered government graves, as just an endless lineage of losers, mere piles of human waste, spending all their time trying to feign some meaning to their lives despite overwhelming evidence that there wasn't any.

Hector felt a burst of panic so intense that his rib cage clamped down on his lungs like a steel vise. *I can't breathe!* His eyes were open, but he couldn't see anything except a sickly green hue. If he hadn't already been leaning against the wall, he would have fallen. He was suffocating out there in the open air under a boundless blue sky. Hector's real prison was a thousand times closer than the fences and guard towers, and right now he felt the whole weight of it, as if all the mammoth limestone blocks supporting the walls of Littonburg had been piled straight onto his chest. Hector thought he was dying right then and there, and not a person on the face of the Earth would know or care. But Monk knew. Hector just couldn't see the truth about Monk. He didn't have the right kind of eyes.

*

After his anxiety attack that day on the yard, Hector couldn't help having a mild curiosity toward Monk. He watched him on the sly as Monk walked down the dingy green cellblock corridor or stood in line at chow hall. He sneaked glances at him as Monk lay on his bed reading his *Peanuts* books, laughing occasionally in an open, happy way like people in prison never laugh. He marveled at Monk's quiet relationship with birds of every description out on the yard, how he meticulously folded crumbs into a napkin after every meal and then mixed them together to create the best bird food he could manage. Hector had never even noticed any birds before, and now they seemed to be everywhere he looked. He also spied what he perceived as an almost incomprehensible loneliness in Monk, a loneliness so deep it frightened Hector; yet at the same time he could see that Monk didn't seem to live *under* his loneliness, but alongside of it, as if his loneliness itself had become a sufficient companion.

And Hector tried subtly from about ten different angles to read that damn little sign over Monk's bed, the one he noticed his first day at Littonburg, but never could manage it.

The more he watched Monk, the more fascinated, almost obsessed, he became with Monk's graceful way of doing things. Despite himself, Hector was finally developing a small flame of hope for his dreary existence, like a drowning man who spots a bright-colored sail way off in the distance. But although they had been neighbors for over two months, Monk and Hector hadn't exchanged a single word.

One night in June just before lockdown, Hector passed by Monk's cell and stole an habitual glance out of the corner of his eye. What he saw stopped him cold. Monk was sitting perfectly straight on his bunk, legs folded in front of him, with an expression on his face that made him look like an angel. Though the light in his cell was off, Monk seemed to be surrounded by an unearthly glow that allowed Hector to see every beatific feature -- his eyes barely closed, eyelids almost imperceptibly fluttering, his mouth slightly open as if in the middle of a sigh, hands turned upward in his lap as though he had let loose his every grip.

Hector's heart felt like it was beating a million times a minute. A deafening silence enveloped him, and USP-Littonburg fell away entirely. Hector had done a lot of good dope in his time and seen a lot of stoned people, but he had never seen anyone look like that, not even in the paintings of saints and angels which adorned the walls of his childhood church in the barrios of Austin, Texas. Over and over he heard, echoing like a huge cathedral in his mind, *AND THE HOLY SPIRIT FILLED THAT PLACE; AND THE HOLY SPIRIT FILLED THAT PLACE; AND THE HOLY SPIRIT FILLED THAT PLACE*, a long-forgotten line from a church service which had stirred his curiosity as a child. Spirit filled the air. He could see it, hear it, even feel it on his breath filling his lungs. He felt like he was filled with light.

Reeling with confusion and wonder, Hector barely managed to make it into his own cell before the locks crashed shut for the night. After so many years of feeling dead, he was suddenly so filled with wonder that he didn't know what to do.

Stretched out flat on his back, hands folded across his chest, Hector lay awake all night gazing blankly at the tiny portion of starry sky visible through the bars of his window. It was the first time he had noticed the stars in as long as he could remember. That night was unique for Hector, not just because of Monk, but also because the particular combination of astonishment and insomnia brought up images of his own life so vividly he couldn't tell whether they were thoughts or hallucinations.

Like most convicts, the crude numbers of Hector's life were way out of whack. At 33, he had spent nearly fifteen years in one joint or another for less than a four-year life of crime. Sometime during that night, he almost laughed when the thought crossed his mind, *I've probably earned more money in dollar-a-day prison jobs than I ever stole from convenience stores anyway.* And he nearly cried when he saw so clearly the depth of his weariness from a life of cops and holding cells and courtrooms and handcuffs too tight against his wristbones.

But the most amazing thing to Hector about that night was the honesty with which he saw himself, as if he were backstage in his own life, looking calmly at the character he had been playing all those years without the innumerable lies, excuses, and the resignation which had become his normal state of mind. What a relief, to be so totally free from the role of Hector Vincantos for awhile!

*

The following morning was another beautiful, pre-summer mountain day. Monk got up from bed slowly, trying to allow the blood to begin circulating in his legs. *It's not often that I sit all night,* he thought. *Good thing, too; It's damn hard on the legs.* Rubbing his ankles and calves slowly with both hands, he had a fleeting thought of Hector. He sensed something had gone on between them, and smiled. He had been waiting months for that play to begin unfolding.

Legs finally working again, Monk walked to the window and looked out at his golden-green morning hills, as he did every day. His eyes fell upon the morning as if he had never seen any of it before, as if there had never *been* a morning before. *God, I love this part of the country! It's so green, so full.* Filling his lungs with delicious, crisp air, Monk closed his eyes and breathed it all in. He took long, deep breaths, like a god, as if to consume the whole outdoors like a tasty breakfast. He breathed in the light, the trees, the wildlife and sounds. He breathed in the morning skies and distant white clouds. He filled himself with extraordinary power. His breath had become a living link to the world, to the whole universe, in which Littonburg was hardly a speck on the map, a brief stopping place along a journey immeasurably vast.

After a time, Monk's daily symphony began. Starting at the far end of the cellblock, perfectly timed and orchestrated, conducted in exactly the same cadence every morning of his life, Monk listened as the sounds grew louder and louder in measured sequence until the crashing crescendo of his own lock opening and then the performance moving down the block, cymbals crashing softer and softer until the final note was played, thirty-one steel doors past his own. Like an evening at a concert, Monk breathed it all in. He felt huge and powerful.

> *The seasons pass; I breathe.*
> *All these faces and forms,*
> *thoughts and dreams,*
> *I breathe. I breathe.*

*

After an unusually hot summer, fall's cool breezes ushered in a good mood across most of the prison, though the early mountain evenings also cut back on yard time and forced the population indoors.

Hector and Monk had become casual friends, Hector finally breaking the ice not long after that night in June when he had seen Monk sitting in perfect peace. Their relationship was strictly small talk, and he certainly wouldn't mention that night to Monk, but not a day had gone by that Hector hadn't pictured the look on Monk's face or the mysterious power he had experienced watching him. And not a night had passed that he hadn't lain in bed longing for the clarity and detachment he had felt toward his own life that same night. And, of course, there was that damn sign over Monk's bed, the sign which Hector still hadn't deciphered and couldn't bring himself to ask Monk about.

On the surface his relationship with Monk didn't look like anything more than would be expected of two people who had to wake up and go to sleep in adjacent cells every day of their lives. They said hello to each other around the prison, exchanged books and magazines, occasionally sat near each other for a few minutes out on the yard. But underneath, a delicate courtship was taking place, though it would be hard to say who was courting whom. Hector was attracted like a moth to a flame, but Monk also had a fundamental need, perhaps the deepest unfulfilled human instinct, to leave something of himself behind in this world -- an emotional or spiritual footprint to guide even a single step of someone else's journey through life.

Inquisitiveness aside, Hector had to proceed cautiously in forging a friendship with an Anglo oldtimer, or at least that's what he imagined. But this wasn't a gang-run Texas State Prison; occasional friendships across racial and cultural lines didn't really matter to anyone here other than Hector. So his mysterious pull toward Monk drove him to take courage he didn't need, to move beyond social taboos which existed only in his mind.

One early October evening, Hector and Monk were leaning against the wall between their cell doors, and Hector summoned the nerve to ask Monk about his life. Hector had held off in several light conversations, but that night his curiosity overcame him. With a motion, Monk invited him into his cell. After a moment's reluctance, Hector broke his own years-long policy and entered a cell other than his own, making a subtle beeline to finally read that silly little sign which had held his attention for months now. It was a crude image of Snoopy, Charlie Brown's dog, hand-drawn on a plain lined sheet of paper scotched-taped to the wall. Snoopy's face had a smile and a wink and the caption above his head said "It's All **Right Here, you know.**"

After so many weeks of curiosity, Hector was quite let down by this. He'd never had a glimmer of what the sign might actually say, but had come to expect something stranger or stronger or more magical than "It's All Right Here, you know." What the hell did that mean anyway?

Meanwhile, Monk sat on his bed, leaned back against the wall and closed his eyes, getting ready to answer Hector's question about his life. "Oh, you know," he began, "it's just a story like anybody else's story."

Hector tore himself away from the sign and took a seat on the floor. Monk continued, "My life didn't start off none too well, I'll tell you. I was state-raised and state-owned. You can call me an old bastard, 'cause that's exactly what I am. My mama was an oil-boom Texas hooker, and *she* was born to a hooker, too. Her life was even rougher than mine, though, 'cause she was *had* the whole time she was growing up by all the 'uncles' who hung out at Granny's. Mama was a cute thing, and Granny loved that little girl a lot, but really there wasn't nothing she could do about that sort of thing back then. Anyways, Mama disappeared pretty early on after dropping me into this world, and I was hustled off from aunt to aunt to granny and back until I was old enough to become a bonafide delinquent in the custody of the Texas Youth Commission."

Hector hadn't expected Monk to start from two generations back, but he wasn't bored. He had never heard Monk speak with such fluidity, this near-silent convict who kept to himself.

Monk tossed Hector his blanket to make the floor a little more comfortable, and continued. "I first made my bones as a convict when I was eighteen, killing two of the three roosters who tried to lay claim to my butt down there in the Colorado State Pen at Canon City. I got off on self-defense, but then ten months later I did the strangest thing: All cool, calm and collected, I walked down to the third guy's cell and shanked him a few hundred times with a rusty bedspring shiv."

Before he could stop himself, Hector exclaimed, "Jesus Christ!"

Monk stopped talking and looked at Hector, neither embarrassed nor reproving. He just looked at him.

Hector felt embarrassed, and said, "I'm sorry, man. It just kinda took me by surprise, you know? I mean, you seem like such a mellow dude..."

"Well, listen," Monk cut in. "You're the one who wanted to know this bullshit."

Still avoiding Monk's eyes, Hector said, "I really had no right to ask; I'm sorry."

Monk said softly, "Listen, Hector, it's okay. I'm just telling you a story. Who cares that it happens to be a true story? Who cares that the story's about me? It's all just a story now."

Hector glanced again at the sign and then down at the floor, understanding less by the minute. Once again speaking from his gut before the mind could restrain him,

Hector looked quickly at Monk and said, "What did it feel like? I mean, to stab the dude hundreds of times... Did you go over the edge?"

Monk resumed his storyteller's position and replied, "Oh, yeah, I went way over the edge. I was totally insane. I felt all this power, like a god. I stabbed and stabbed the poor son of a bitch for three or four minutes, long after I knew he was dead. I even got angrier when the body stopped twitching. I didn't want it to be done yet."

Over the next two hours, Hector gradually opened his mind and heart to Monk as he never had before to anyone. He let go every vestige of inhibition. The storyteller and listener became like two parts of one mind; questions and reactions flowed back and forth like water.

"I've never killed anybody," Hector confided, "but I know what you're talking about. I mean about being totally insane."

Monk said, "Everybody, somewhere deep in their bones, knows that feeling. I'll tell you, you can't beat the thrill of real madness, you know, when you're out there, finally doing whatever the hell you want to with nary a shred of reason, guilt, doubt, or fear of what's gonna happen to you. It's like... like being God, I guess. I can understand why some guys never come out of it. After all, there's a kind of peace of mind to being crazy. Anyway, when the guards finally came I was cooperative and casual, sitting perfectly relaxed next to this bloody rag doll that had been a human being just a few minutes before."

Monk paused reflectively, then said, "I was pretty crazy, but not crazy enough to want to stand trial for murder one. And John Law, well he don't really care when convicts knock off convicts anyway. It's like free pest control to him.

So they let me cop a plea for voluntary manslaughter, and I got fifty-five years on top of my original fifteen for armed robbery and my nickel for grand theft auto. I didn't even *see* the board until I was thirty-four years old, and they didn't kick me loose 'til a few years after that."

Hector said, "So you did nearly twenty years straight time?"

"Eighteen years three-and-a-half months, boy. And then I was in the federal slammer less than a year later for bank robbery."

Hector and Monk both laughed. That last part was certainly familiar -- the convict's great mystery, like an undiscovered fourth law of motion: what comes out, goes back in.

Monk went on to describe how over the next dozen years, he had been in and out of prisons all over the country. By his reckoning, he had robbed twenty-seven banks and had only been caught for eight of them, so he was way ahead in the cops-and-robbers game. Though on the streets he flaunted every law possible, in prison he lived by the Code and knew how to do his time.

He explained to Hector that although he really did enjoy his interludes of freedom, "Hell, I'd nearly *break* back in after seven or eight months on the street. After all, I never felt at ease in the free world, and prison was a society in which I'd already become a well-respected citizen, a success. As long as I could get used to lookin' at cute boys instead of cute girls, it hasn't been such a bad life. At least I understood the rules."

But somewhere along the line things changed for James Ray Dodds. And though it didn't happen in a blinding flash of light or divine revelation, still there was one identifiable

100

moment, a turning point, that he wouldn't understand or recognize until many years afterward. He told that part of the story when Hector asked him about the scars on his throat.

"Pure and simple," Monk replied, "I slit my throat. I had just been sentenced to natural life in Texas under the Habitual Criminal Act. Being from Texas, you know that's the only sentence that really and truly means I'd never set foot outside again. Well I thought, *Cops and robbers is over, and the robbers done lost. I ain't gonna let these turkeys watch me get old and gray. No ma'am, thanks all the same.* I just took hold of a razor blade and went at it. I damn near died too, but in a funny way it worked out pretty well. The TDC sick bay was so overcrowded, they transferred me into the federal system under the Interstate Compact and shipped me out to the medical facility at Springfield. My sentence didn't change, but I'll tell you, natural life here with the feds is a whole different century than hard labor in them cotton fields around Huntsville."

Monk gazed out his window for a moment, as if he could see himself out in those cotton field gun crews, the hot Texas sun sapping his lifeblood away hour by hour, day by day, for years on end. He looked back at Hector, and Hector could see profound compassion in his eyes, perhaps for all the Monks and Hectors whom fate hadn't rescued from those cotton fields. Startled and a little embarrassed by Monk's sudden emotional depth, Hector looked away after a moment.

"Anyway, as they were wheeling me out of TDC on a stretcher to the transport bus, this old, leather-skinned trusty seemed to appear out of nowhere. I found out later his name was Eli. Well, old Eli, he looked down at me with soft eyes that didn't seem to have no bottom to 'em at all, and he pressed the palm of his right hand right here against the center of my chest. It was the strangest thing I ever felt. I can't even explain it now, after all these years."

Hector immediately thought, *Oh yeah, well the strangest thing I ever felt was when you were sitting right here on your bed last June...* , but he said nothing.

"So I'm laying there," Monk continued, "and it was like everything stood still for I don't know how long. I couldn't see nothing but his eyes, and finally Eli just pats my chest a little with that big old hand of his and says 'It's all right here, you know,' and gives me a big smile."

Hector briefly glanced back to the sign on the wall, but said nothing. This was way out of his league, and he didn't especially want to hear Monk's answers to any questions he might have about what it all meant. Hector's life had no room for mysteries. Mysteries implied surprise, they implied curiosity and hope -- all luxuries of the free, not essentials in the defeated life of a three-time loser.

Monk went on, "Then Eli said, 'Listen son, natural life ain't the end. It just means you're a monk now, 'stead of a civilian waiting to go home. You got a home now. You ain't never gonna have no mortgage or alimony or bills to pay, never gonna worry about kids, or your wife cheatin' on you. You and me, we don't have to give up nothin' to be monks. It's all right here, you know. We just gotta learn how to use the time. Now you take care of yourself, monk.'"

"Damndest stuff I ever heard, at least back then. With my neck still all bandaged up I couldn't talk even if I had something to say, which I surely didn't. In fact, I was hardly listening. The look in that old man's eyes, and the strength in his hand, had all my attention. To tell you the truth, I had no idea what was going on, but whatever it was, I didn't really care to think about it right then. My circuits was all blown."

Hector understood every word Monk said about that experience with Eli, because of his own feelings that night in June. He still hadn't told Monk about that, but knew somehow that he didn't need to. Sticking to the sequence of Monk's story, Hector said, "So that's when you started calling yourself Monk?"

Monk responded, "Well, now there's another funny thing. The bus hacks, who didn't know me at all, heard Eli say 'You take care of yourself, monk.' So they thought Monk must be my nickname, and by the time the bus arrived in Missouri five days later, so did all the other convicts aboard. I still couldn't talk for another week until I got my stitches out. When I did start to talk again, hell, everyone in the joint called me Monk, and I didn't really care enough to try to straighten it all out."

Over the next few evenings Monk continued his story as if he and Hector were sitting around a fire somewhere, two cowpoke buddies on a long distance cattle drive, or two ancient tribal hunters entertaining each other at night. He told of how he gradually lightened up over the next several years after arriving in Springfield. He had spent most of his time alone and quiet. He removed himself from the usual prison games -- power, fear, greed, frustration, bravado, regrets, fantasies. He became the fool on the hill, enjoying birdsong and sunshine, gazing fondly out on the plains of Missouri, then the dogwoods around Atlanta, then the mountains around Littonburg. And Hector, listening, could see the sights, smell the fragrances and hear the sounds Monk described.

One evening Hector said, "But how can you enjoy your life so much? I mean, you're still stuck in here for good, man."

Monk thought for a minute, trying to choose the right words, and said, "Well, like ol' Snoopy over there says, 'it's all right here, you know'. I'm not comparing being here with being on the street. I don't compare the people here to anybody else I ever knew -- and even if I did, hell, you're a damn sight better friend than the characters I hung out with out there. But I mean, what's the point? Here is where I am, and I feel pretty good. This is my life, Hector. I'm healthy, I live in the mountains, I have enough to eat, I stay warm. You're the one with a burden; you still have the streets waiting for you. There's all sorts of shit you have to think about and figure out. This is my world right here."

Hector cut in, "You also have assholes with clubs telling you when you can eat, looking up your ass with a flashlight, and whatever else they want to do."

Monk smiled. "Hector, I don't know if you ever noticed, but there's no shortage of assholes on the street. This whole world seems to breed a fair number of assholes, if you think about it. It's like weeds or something. And hell, I hear people pay pretty good money to have folks shine lights up their asses." Hector couldn't help but laugh, and Monk joined him. Monk was right on target, and Hector was just beginning to understand how Monk had somehow torn down all the prison walls in his own mind, and saw the world as one world, not inside versus outside.

But Hector didn't understand more than a glimmer of it. Long ago when Monk truly accepted that he was never getting out, he cut all his ties -- not only to the free world, but even to past and future. He had no greater ambition than to make the most of each day. He turned his attention to simple things: the immensity of the sky, changes in the weather, the sensation of his own breath flowing in and out like the breath of the whole universe.

Though in everyone else's mind he had become severely institutionalized, Monk had actually gained Spirit, not lost it. He slowly discovered great peace waiting quietly within himself as he removed all the chaos that had covered it up for so long. Like Eli -- and in some mysterious way partly *because* of Eli -- Monk became a calm, sane man in an insane environment, an initiate in an ironic lineage of inner freedom which gradually dwarfed the puny restrictions imposed by concrete and steel.

One crisp October day out on the yard, Monk and Hector sat together watching a few migrating birds cautiously approach Monk's napkin full of scraps. Hector looked across the yard and saw Teddy Anthimos doing benchpress with Paco, Raoul and Carlos Charlie spotting him and hanging out together. "Sorry son of a bitch," Hector said as he indicated Teddy by a turn of his head, "blind as a bat for good."

Monk replied, "It might just be, you know."

Hector said "What do you mean?"

"Well, a few months ago young Teddy over there was ornery from morning to night and didn't have a real friend in the world. Now look at him. His blindness gentled the hell out of him, it seems to me; and your friends over there really care about him."

Hector couldn't hear it. "Are you loco, man? You mean to tell me it's all right he went blind?"

Monk replied, "I'm just making an observation. Don't be so sure of what you think or what you see, Hector. Life's funny that way. I mean, what was supposed to happen to Teddy? Stay pissed off all his life and go down someday in a fight over a pack of smokes? Is that what's so important for his eyes to see?"

Hector looked back at the weight bench. Carlos Charlie had just told a joke of some sort and the guys were all laughing, Teddy included. This was new territory for Hector, and he didn't especially like the spiritual challenge Monk was laying at his feet. "Shit, man, I'll see you back on the block. I'm getting cold out here."

*

By mid-autumn, as the chilly evening sky cut yard time progressively shorter and Hector's chicano compadres had to relocate from the workout area to one of the television dayrooms, Hector -- still playing out his imaginary social games -- discreetly began returning to his tier early enough to drop by Monk's cell for a couple of hours before lockdown. There was a quality about their meetings that drew Hector in more deeply every day. In that squalid little cell in the middle of nowhere, he could feel civilized, even worthwhile, in a way he had never felt before. As much as Monk meant to him as a sort of father-figure, Hector also felt appreciated for improving on Monk's loneliness -- though the loneliness had a depth to it which Hector knew he couldn't touch.

As time went by, there was really no other place he wanted to be. By January, the month of Hector's thirty-fourth birthday, he was spending every evening talking quietly with the first real friend of his life. He knew that he had now been chalked up as an oldtimer, but it no longer mattered. He had never felt younger.

One night Hector and Monk were playing gin on the bed in Hector's cell -- another surrender of policy for Hector -- when he asked Monk why he didn't have any other friends.

"Well, actually I consider Freddy a close friend. You know, friends aren't always the people you see or talk to the most."

"You mean Skinny Freddy?", asked Hector.

"Yeah, I do. He's a good friend. We understand each other perfectly."

This tack was a little too weird for Hector, who immediately felt threatened by things he didn't understand, so he said, "Well, I guess I'm talking more about.. you know, someone like me, who uh.. who talks and everything."

Monk replied, "Oh, you mean like a pardner. Yeah, Freddy's a good friend, but he's nobody's pardner. Well, I'm just a one-pard'-at-a-time sort of guy, I guess. Always have been."

Hector asked who the "pardner" was before himself.

"Ah, let's see; I guess that would be Robin, Robin Foster, left here about two years ago. Stayed right here in your cell, too."

Hector could feel a story coming on, so he folded his gin hand and settled back to hear it.

"Robin was cool, boy; I mean naturally cool. He wasn't a very deep person, mind you, and he made pretty bad decisions all his life, but he was sharp! And he had a great sense of humor, even when he didn't know it."

Hector was intrigued, yet at the same time felt a twinge of jealousy at the affectionate playfulness Monk seemed to enjoy so much in his friendship with this Robin Foster. It was that lightness, that humorousness, which Hector envied most about Monk. And in all those months it hadn't seemed to rub off on Hector at all. He was still heavy; his lightest moods might be described as neutral, while his depressions were frequent and intense.

Monk continued, "Yeah, Robin was great. Even the prosecutors had to admit his last big scam was brilliant. And the first time he told me about it, I laughed myself to tears; I chuckled out loud for days every time I thought about it." Monk was back several years in the past now, hearing Robin himself telling his story with youthful exuberance.

"Okay, picture this," Robin had said, "a machine-shop quality steel box about four feet high, two feet wide, and two feet deep. I made it myself. Now dig, it was completely smooth and closed except for an envelope depository slot on the front of it just under the top edge. I painted the box blue and gray *exactly* like First Union's buildings, tellers' uniforms and their logo-thing. I mean, Mrs. Union herself couldn't've spotted the difference."

"All right," he continued, "so then I made an equally 'perfecto' sign that says: NIGHT DROP OUT OF ORDER; PLEASE USE TEMPORARY REPLACEMENT DEPOSITORY." Robin paused and looked at Monk. "Are you following this, man?"

"Oh yeah," Monk replied, "I love it. Go on, go on."

"Okay, so then I steal a handtruck from K-Mart by just walking out with it, you know, like I was a delivery man or something. Don't forget, this son of a bitchin' box I made weighs about 200 pounds. Anyway, about once every two weeks, just after dark, I load the sucker into the back of my pickup and drive to a First Union branch. In about ten minutes, the box is in place, I hang the sign on the real depository and take off. No alarms, no break-in, no security, nothin'. Just about ten minutes of luck and the rest is history. Of course, I do have to wake up early, which is kind of a drag, but hell, life's a bitch, right?"

Monk smiled with fatherly affection at this enterprising young man.

"So around six the next morning, I pick up my props, lock myself in the garage, remove the bolts from the bottom of the box, and count my loot. I rode back by during the day and deposited all the checks, man, 'cause I don't need that bullshit, and I figured it would take 'em longer to realize what was going on that way. I only kept the cash, change, traveller's checks and money orders."

Robin was really buzzing just from telling his story. He was proud of his undetected, nonviolent bank robberies and he made quite a decent living at it for nearly two years. Nothing to retire on, but enough to enjoy life without working.

Monk said, "So what are you doing here?"

Robin shook his head and laughed. "I fucking overslept, man. I overslept. I tied one on after I done the set-up one night, and the next morning I opened my eyes and it was 8 a.m. Now, the bank opened at 8:30. So I threw some clothes on, hopped into the pickup and tried to beat the clock. Of course, forgetting the goddamn handtruck didn't help. Can you imagine how suprised the bank manager was to pull into the parking lot at 8:23 in the morning and see this crazy dude sweating and struggling to get the depository box into a pickup truck? I'll tell you, though, everybody was *very* impressed, including the FBI agents. They grilled me for about an hour trying to get me to admit that these 'ingenious' -- I swear to God, that was the word -- bank jobs must have been pulled to finance some fancy-ass terrorist group."

Robin had paused, turning reflective suddenly, and looked out the barred window into empty sky. "Man, that was a great scam, Monk, it really was. If I never do another thing, I did that one right, man. It was righteous."

Monk looked with wonder at that upbeat young man who under different circumstances might have become a great engineer or executive, and thought, *He's close to tears at the beauty of his scam; I love this crazy dude!*

Monk enjoyed Robin a lot for a couple of years. He was what he was, and a happy one at that. But like most other friends Monk would ever make, Robin did his time and was released. Monk would be there forever.

His reverie over, Monk reentered the present and looked at Hector. By then Hector was more touched by Monk's affection for Robin than he was jealous of it, and he said, "So do you ever hear from him, man? What's he doing now?"

"Nah," Monk answered, "He's got a whole new world now; he's got no business with me anymore." Monk made that statement without the slightest melancholy or self-pity, and Hector was struck with awe for this unlikely wise man who seemed so free of even the most acceptable attachments and burdens which weigh most people down.

From time to time Monk taught Hector subtle ways of breathing or of sitting perfectly still and focusing the mind on silence. Nothing very formal, but tips gleaned from many years of listening to silence and of looking at himself with extraordinary honesty. Hector was beginning to loosen up and feel lighter. But their friendship was not without its lapses. A few times when he and Monk laughed loudly at something or other, Hector panicked at the sound of his own laughter. It was too unlike his entire conception of himself. When that happened, Hector usually entered a period of depression during which he avoided Monk. Instead of their nightly conversations, he would score some pot from Paco and lie on his bunk stoned without moving an inch for twelve or fourteen hours at a time.

Some nights he would lie awake all night trying unsuccessfully to recapture the calm, detached state of mind he had experienced that night in June. But the pot made him unable to focus, and in frustration he simply smoked more at those times, until he would finally drop off in a stupor and sleep most of the day. Like Monk and many of the other inmates on D-block, especially the older ones, Hector wasn't involved in any educational or vocational training programs, and he was far down on the waiting list of 1200 men for 200 institutional jobs. All his time was his own -- a dream to the average working stiff out on the streets, but a nightmare to a depressed convict.

During his depressions he sometimes even considered dropping his friendship with Monk, but deep in his gut he knew that Monk was the most fearless person he had ever met, and he desperately wanted some of that fearlessness.

*

Three years passed, and Hector slowly changed, much like James Ray Dodds had changed thirty years earlier. By living next to Monk, he came to see that truth isn't found in books, and that happiness can't be seized by force. He eased off from his constant demands and aversions, and the lines around his eyes softened. He spoke less and listened more, and the corners of his mouth loosened up. He looked much younger at 36 than when he had gotten to Littonburg at 33. Of course, there was still something, some invisible punch line, that Hector knew he hadn't picked up yet from Monk. Hector was still quite a serious soul. He longed to experience Monk's light, playful relationship to life.

One freezing night toward the end of winter, a month or so after his thirty-seventh birthday, Hector returned to his cell after dinner to see why Monk hadn't made it to chow. Monk wasn't in his cell. Hector checked the dayroom, but he wasn't there either. The library was closed, no movies or special programs were scheduled, and there just wasn't any other place to look.

Hector's puzzlement turned quickly to concern and was well on its way to becoming full-blown panic. He felt a sense of abandonment he hadn't felt since his father disappeared without a trace when Hector was nine years old. Hector asked a guard whether he had seen Monk, and the guard replied only that he was in sick bay; he didn't know why.

Hector felt all the cruelty and oppression of prison life once again. He wasn't allowed to rush across the yard to find out what had happened to his only friend, and the guards didn't care enough to find out for him. He returned to his cell more dumbfounded than angry, as though he had looked out his window and the mountains themselves were gone. He didn't know what to do.

Hector scored some pot and smoked until he dropped off into a stupor sometime in the middle of the night. He slept fitfully, in jerks and snatches, bombarded by a barrage of psychedelic dreams. In one, he was a young child again, five or six years old, waiting in line with his mother and older sister to see Santa Claus in a dingy little department store in San Antonio. When it came time for him to sit on

Santa's lap, he looked into the man's face and saw Monk smiling at him. Though there was great love in Monk's eyes, Hector was terrified. Santa/Monk held little Hector back from running away, and teased, "It's all right here, you know."

In another dream, Hector was back on the bus with Shabazz and Marion Justice. Justice was cursing at Shabazz relentlessly and then began to beat him. Hector screamed in frustration and anger as he struggled unsuccessfully to break the ring which linked his handcuffs to the arm of his seat. All the other convicts stared straight ahead in silence, as did Harvey Hewlitt, the driver. Hector was shrieking by now, "You sonofabitch, you're killing him!" when suddenly Shabazz and Justice both turned toward him and said in unison, as blood dripped off both sides of Shabazz's face, "It's all right here, you know."

Hector awoke from that dream shortly before daybreak, nearly paralyzed with fear and moaning loudly enough to elicit angry catcalls from three or four adjacent cells. He lay awake until the morning din began and then crossed his cell to splash cold water on his face. As he dried off with a dirty t-shirt, he heard Monk's cell door open and Hector sprang to life with a sense of great relief. But his relief died quickly into terrible grief when he saw two officers routinely tossing Monk's few possessions into a black plastic garbage bag. Hector spoke before he could stop himself. "What're you doing?"

Only one officer turned to respond, "The old man died last night. You got anything in here belongs to you, you'd better grab it now; he don't need it any more, and the rest of this stuff'll get dumped."

Stunned, Hector moved listlessly back into his cell.

Within a few minutes, Monk's worldly possessions -- mostly *Peanuts* books -- were cleared out and the guards had gone. Hector stood in front of Monk's cell staring at the past, seeing himself and his only friend talking, joking, relaxing, making so many hundreds of days and nights more endurable. After a while Hector turned to go, when out of the corner of his eye he caught sight of that curious little sign, the only one of Monk's possessions left behind in the cleanup. With a quick look to both sides like a child about to cross the street without permission, Hector stole in and tenderly lifted the sign off the wall. Tears streaming silently down his face, he returned to his own cell, taped it to the wall across from his bed, and entered into the worst depression of his life.

*

Over the next three years, Hector didn't stay straight long enough to think much about Monk or about how his own life had begun to open up back then. Even the dreams stopped trying to remind him after a while, except for once or twice a year when he would dream of Monk and invariably wake up crying over the friendship he missed so terribly.

He lost weight and let his appearance go to hell, since the only commodities he could sell for dope money were his food and toiletries furnished by the government. He slept through one annual parole hearing and showed up stoned for another. He was no longer looking for good breaks or friends or dignity or mentors. He wouldn't have recognized another Monk or Shabazz if he walked right into one. Raoul, Paco, and Carlos Charlie had all been released. Teddy Anthimos had been transferred to the Medical Facility at Springfield after being beaten nearly to death by two young angel-dust freaks. Skinny Freddy and Brother

Malcolm were the only cons in the cell block who were still there from the time Hector first arrived, and Hector had never had a conversation with either of them.

And today, Skinny Freddy was maxing out. Not having spoken a word in all these years, he remained a legendary figure of sorts, and dozens of inmates now took the liberty of approaching him to offer heartfelt good wishes for his life on the street. Skinny Freddy would listen intently to each one, and then offer his famous cosmic smile and a two-handed handshake which spoke volumes of affection. He looked like a mime running for president. As Hector noticed all this he thought, *Strange scene, man,* and he tried to hide from himself the pain he felt on seeing all those genuine expressions of caring.

Later in the afternoon, Skinny Freddy was being escorted down the hallway for the last time. Congratulations and goodbyes echoed his footsteps as he glided down the tier. When he came to Hector's cell, he stopped so abruptly that the officer behind him slammed into his back. Skinny Freddy looked at Hector sitting on the edge of his bunk, looked at him as if he could see right through his soul. Hector hadn't looked directly into anyone's eyes since Monk had died, but now he gazed steadily back, feeling a stirring of aliveness like clear, cool water in the desert. Hector rose and came to his doorway, equally puzzled and anxious. Layers and layers of resistance fell off in a continuing stream, and his puzzlement turned to astonishment when he realized that Skinny Freddy was about to say something!

In a soft voice no one in the prison had ever heard, Skinny Freddy said, "Monk knew the truth, friend. He didn't die, he just finished up." Then he smiled that grin which had no equal, and placed his big, bony hand on

Hector's chest and continued, "It's all right here, you know." He just stood there for a minute with his hand on Hector just as Monk had long ago described his own encounter with Eli. Hector felt the tiniest vibration in the center of his chest, and Freddy's eyes seemed to smile right into that same place. Then with Hector stunned into silence and the guard following in a daze, Skinny Freddy sidled off down the hall to his new life outside the walls.

Hector didn't know what to make of all this. He hadn't felt this way since that night in June nearly seven years ago when he saw Monk in ecstasy. He paced for a while, then sat on his bunk, then gradually closed his eyes and felt his shortness of breath in the midst of all this anxiety. He remembered a conversation he once had with Monk after Hector's rejection by the parole board, something curious Monk had said about "dealing with the feelings": "Hector, the strongest feelings we have -- positive or negative, it don't matter -- are keys to the kingdom, boy; they're keys to the kingdom. Every single thing you feel is power. The stronger the feeling, the more power. Don't fritter it away by pacing the floor or pounding the wall or biting your nails off or bashing somebody's head in. What you do is *feel* it; feel the whole thing by sitting perfectly still and not moving a muscle. What is this confusion? What is this anger? What is this worry? What do they feel like in your gut and your heart and mind? What's behind 'em, just out of reach, that gives 'em so much power? You see, Hector, at some point you get tired of being the puppet on a string, and you decide to catch the punch line."

Hector still couldn't make much sense of it, but now there seemed nothing else to do. He took control of his breathing, and made it slower and deeper. He sat for an hour, then two, then he adjusted his position a little to let his back rest against the wall. When he tried to feel the anxiety as Monk had suggested, it seemed to keep slipping out of sight. He went through periods of feeling nothing at all, then feeling guilt for feeling nothing, then back into the feelings again -- the cycles came and went for many hours.

At dawn, as he felt the light filter gently through his closed eyelids, Hector realized that he had sat perfectly still all night, and chuckled at how bizarre that would have seemed to him just a few days ago. He felt very calm. Now he vividly remembered his first sight of Monk in ecstasy, and that strange glimpse of Monk and Skinny Freddy bowing to each other with mystical respect. *They knew something, they really did.* And with a mixture of excitement and fear Hector thought, *Someday, someday...*, and smiled a smile nearly as big as Skinny Freddy's.

In the center of his chest, he felt a warm glow of gratitude for the outlandish turn of events which led him to this point. Who was that strange old monk who had stolen his way so deeply into Hector's heart, who seemed to steal his misery and self-pity bit by bit like a cunning thief? And who was that other bizarre figure, who broke many years of silence to remind him of his teacher, of his lineage and his journey?

The more he thought of Monk and Skinny Freddy, the more love he felt, a pulsing force in the center of his chest that seemed large enough to hold all the universe within it. How could he bemoan even the pain and struggle in his life, when it took all of that to lead him to such unlikely saints in this deformed monastery of the absurd? *How could I have any regrets? Every moment has been perfect. Every moment has been perfect.*

Something very deep wrenched open inside Hector's chest, and in that place, echoing louder and louder, *was EVERY MOMENT HAS BEEN PERFECT!* Hector's mind cracked apart like a coconut. *Oh, my God, that's what was behind Monk's playfulness and humor: It was all perfect, every horrible step along the way; every bad decision, everything I thought was an accident, all those years of depression, the times I held on by my fingernails to my last shred of sanity. All perfect! Just a stage-play. Oh, my God, my God!*

Hector's mind and heart burst into a million pieces. Tears streamed down his face in ecstasy, though he wasn't aware of them at all. His mouth hung open, his eyelids fluttered, and his breath stopped. He was aware only of the Light, the Light all around him, the Light within him, the Light which surpassed a thousand suns. He became Love, the stuff from which everything else is made, beyond space and time, beyond the agony of suffering or the bliss of pleasure, beyond the birth and death of the frail bodies we so briefly possess.

Every fear, every unhappiness left him, having burst into nothingness like so many soap bubbles which seem huge but turn out to be hollow inside. He had finally caught the punch line. Hector opened his eyes for the first time all night, and immediately focused on the yellowed little sign which he had never yet understood. Now Snoopy seemed to be smiling brighter, and the words singing off the page, "It's all **right** here, you know; it's **all** right here, you know; it's **all** right **here**, you know." And Hector marveled at how simple the truth turned out to be after such a long way around. He closed his eyes again, and smiled Skinny Freddy's smile and laughed Monk's laugh, under his breath, like the sweet mystic madman he had finally become.

Epilogue

There was a new transfer on the cellblock that same day, a broken man whose cell faced Hector's. Merle Jackson was a large white man with shaved head and full red beard, whose eyes seemed haunted with humiliation and secrecy to an extreme uncommon even in this fortress of the damned. Merle hadn't been able to sleep this first night at Littonburg, and hearing some movement in Hector's cell, he happened to be watching at sunrise as Hector entered the Great Mystery.

Merle had never seen anyone look like that in his whole life, and he couldn't get it out of his mind. He had spent years practicing isolation in order to protect himself and his dangerous secret, but within a few days Merle struck up a conversation with Hector on the yard. It had been many years, and Merle didn't realize he had ever met Hector before. But someday, at the right time, Hector would let Merle know that he recognized Marion Justice underneath that heavier frame, beard and shaved head, and that he forgave him his past. Someday, at the right time, that compassionate revelation would turn Merle's whole life around in a heartbeat.

For now, the two men did their time together as had Monk and Hector. Each night Merle could be seen sitting on the floor in Hector's cell while Hector sat on the bed, neither of them noticing the classic picture they made of master and disciple breathing life into an unbroken lineage of true freedom as the shadows of prison bars moved slowly across their faces.

I see the road now, I'm coming home.
Teach me to sit still, to love life,
To move beyond you into the One.
Where have I been hiding all this time?

The End

DANNY'S DAD

*An original one-act play
performed by Bo & Josh Lozoff
at the Burbage Theater in Los Angeles
in June, 1992.*

DANNY'S DAD

The visiting room of a maximum-security state prison somewhere in the Southwest U.S. This is "minimum-contact visiting," which means that inmates and their visitors enter from different doors into an area in which inmates sit at a counter on one side of a wire-mesh partition and their visitors on the other. Whereas "No-contact visiting" separates the two by glass or industrial plastic and communication must take place by telephone, this level of visiting permits flat-hand touching on the mesh and direct speaking in normal tones of voice. Visitors must empty all the contents of their pockets into safekeeping before entry, and inmates must subject themselves to a full "strip-search," including the inspection of body cavities and orifices, upon entering and exiting the visiting area. Visitors are permitted to bring in one pack of cigarettes and one book of matches, both purchased on site from a machine in the sign-in area.

DANNY is seen sitting on the visitor's side in a metal chair, fidgeting, occasionally biting his fingernails. He is a Native American teenager, seventeen or eighteen, who would be more handsome if he didn't look so lost and angry. He is well-built, wearing a T-shirt to expose his muscular arms, with a pack of cigarettes tucked under the sleeve of his right arm, and one cigarette which he has just this moment placed behind his right ear. Throughout the play he fidgets with his pack of cigarettes.

The prisoners' door finally opens. TAG enters hesitantly, scans the long partition and spots DANNY. All in a moment his face shows relief, affection, degradation, and nervousness. He hasn't seen his son for nearly two years. TAG is a Native American in his mid-forties whose eyes reveal both depth and pain. His hair is military-short. DANNY reacts visibly to his father's appearance, startled by his hair and rattled by how much smaller a man he seems than DANNY *remembered.* TAG *gulps down his discomfort and speaks as he begins to move toward the visiting table.*

TAG: Oh my God, I ain't believin' this! Danny, you're a man! You're beautiful! Look at you!

DANNY: Yeah, well, y'know, it's been awhile.

TAG: You really are beautiful, man; a beautiful young man. Jeez, look at you.

DANNY: They cut your hair?

TAG: What do you think? Pretty strange, huh? [*Danny reacts*] Hey, it'll grow back, give it a few years —

DANNY: How come? How come they cut it? I seen other guys with long hair, I even saw a guy with a braid like yours.

TAG: It's no big deal. I mean Jeez, I've got my son here! And look at you! [*uncomfortable pause...*] So how are you? What's happening in your life?

DANNY: Nothing. Nothing much. Just hanging out, y'know.

TAG: Who you hanging out with these days?

DANNY: Just some guys. You wouldn't know 'em.

TAG: What kind of guys? What are you into?

DANNY: Nothing! What are you, a cop?

TAG: [*hurt*] No, I don't seem to be a cop, do I?

DANNY: I'm sorry, I mean, it's just that I get this shit from Mom and Willie all the time. All they want to know is where I'm going, what I'm doing, who I'm doing it with, how I met them. Jesus, I'm not doing anything. I'm just hanging out.

TAG: You getting along okay with this guy Willie? He ain't knocking you around or anything, is he?

DANNY: Shit, I could kick his ass to Texas and back, Dad [TAG *reacts with some degree of pride*]. Nah, he's just in my face the same as Mom.

TAG: They're probably just trying to be good parents, Danny.

DANNY: He's not my father; he's *her* husband.

TAG: Yeah, I think I know that. [DANNY *reacts to having said the wrong thing again so soon; slight pause while Tag tries to shift gears*] Hey, how's Grandpa Joe? You go up and see him?

DANNY: Sometimes. I don't know, couple times a year, I guess.

TAG: Is he okay — you know, all of this and everything?

DANNY: He took it pretty hard when you went away, and then when she got married...he took sick for a long time, but now he's okay. He says he watches over you.

TAG: I really miss that old man.

DANNY: He wants me to do a vision quest. Up on the mountain, alone for five days.

TAG: Yeah? You going to?

DANNY: I don't know; probably not.

TAG: [*putting his right hand flat against the wire mesh*] Hey, come on, remember? Let's see. [*Danny hesitates, then raises his left hand to meet his father's, digit for digit. Their first touch in two years. Tag reacts, softly:*] ...Wow. You've caught up with me, kid. [*pause while hands continue touching, Tag's hand almost imperceptibly trying to caress his son's.*]

DANNY: [*awkwardly bringing hand away from mesh*] What size shoes?

TAG: Eight-and-a-half. How about you?

DANNY: Nine.

TAG: I really can't believe it. And look at that body! Been working out too, huh?

DANNY: Not much anymore. I was heavy into it last year.

TAG: Play any sports at school?

DANNY: Nah. School sucks.

TAG: What are you talking about? You used to love school!

DANNY: Let's just say I wised up. [*DANNY deftly removes cigarette from behind his ear, taps it on the counter, and lights up*]

TAG: [*finally exasperated*] Aw, come on, man! What's going on with you? I keep trying to talk to you and you're cutting me off at the knees. You know, if I wanted to hang out with stupid young fucks with a bad attitude, I could've stayed out there on the yard; there's a *bunch* of that shit out there.

DANNY: Well, if *I* wanted a lecture about my attitude, I could've stayed home. There's a bunch of *that* shit back there.

.....Wait a minute! Is that what this whole visit is about? Did *she* set this whole thing up?

TAG: What are you talking about? I wanted to see you.

DANNY: Don't bullshit me, man! Answer my question! Was this her idea? Does she expect you to straighten me out?

TAG: Hey, you're my son!

DANNY: Then answer me, damn it! [TAG *motions for* DANNY *to restrain himself in those surroundings;* DANNY *lowers his volume but spits his words out between his teeth*] For two years you didn't want me to see you in here, didn't want me to see you like this, and now suddenly it's okay with you and okay with her, and even Willie is saying "Yeah, you really should go see your old man." She wrote you, didn't she? Yes or no! Was this visit her idea?! Yes or no?!

TAG: [*pauses*] Yeah, it was her idea, but...

DANNY: [*grabbing his cigarettes and rising, walking toward door*] You didn't even want to see me. I'm out of here, man.

TAG: [*frantically*] Danny, get back here! Please kid, don't leave me like this! If they open that door, that's it! Please get back here, quick! I'm begging you...[DANNY *torn apart, grudgingly returns to his seat and looks straight down at the floor. TAG gathers his thoughts, gropes for a new beginning.*] Look at me, look me right in the eyes. Danny, please. I'll never bullshit you, I swear. Look at me, please. [*pause. TAG begins, searching for each word from the depths of his heart.*] The first day I got here, that was the awfulest day of my life. I sat down in the middle of the floor in my cell and cried my eyes out. Then I faced to the east, and I asked the sun to always light your path, and your mom's, and Grandpa Joe's. Then I turned my face north so you could all move on without me. I thought that was the right thing. But you think I haven't missed you? Are you crazy?? I swear I've missed you every day of my life in here. I felt like somebody ripped my heart out. Two years, Danny, two years without a word...

DANNY: Yeah, I know exactly how long it's been.

TAG: [*verging on anger*] Two years in <u>this</u> place, Danny! Without a word! [*pause, calms down*] ...And then a couple months back your mom writes me. She says Danny's cutting school, staying out all night, hanging out with tough guys, mouthing off to her...

DANNY: I'm not doing anything wrong! They're just on me all the time for nothing!

TAG: Maybe they're *on* you because they don't want you to wind up in a place like this! Jesus Christ, kid! You know, *you're* the one who begged us all your life to move off the reservation so you could go to a "regular" American school and live in a "regular" American city like a "regular" American kid! We left Grandpa Joe and the elders for you. I sweated blood to save up money for that house! I drove back-to-back cross-country rigs, I even...[*catches himself, but too late*]...I worked my ass off for you...

DANNY: You what? You carried coke for me? You're here because of me?

TAG: I didn't say that. I...

DANNY: Yes you did! Yes you did! That's exactly what you said!

TAG: I didn't *mean* it that way...

128

DANNY: [*chafing at the need for restraint*] It's bullshit, man! *I'm* not the one who hauled coke in his fucking semi, and *I'm* not the one who got fucking remarried just because you got busted. It's bullshit. You're here because of me, Mom and Willie argue because of me, I'm not doing shit, man. I get blamed for everything, and I'm not doing shit.

[*long pause, both not knowing how to get out of this nightmare*]

TAG: Danny, please. I *really* don't want things to go bad between us. [*Holds both his hands up palms outward toward Danny, but not touching the mesh*] Here: I am sorry to my bones for being such a stupid asshole and messing up our lives like I did. Okay? I'm sorry. I'm sorry. I'm sorry! I'm not blaming you, okay? None of it's your fault. If I could take it back I would. If I could cut my fucking heart out to set things straight for you, I would Danny, I swear. But I'm getting out of here in a couple of years, do you think I want to pass you on the bus coming in? I need you, Danny. I lost my wife, I lost my rig. I really need to be your dad.

DANNY: (*softer*) You'll always be my dad.

TAG: Then *talk* to me. Please. It's important. This is the whole rest of your life we're talking about. *You're* important. Look around. Go on, look around at this place! This is no joke. This is real.

[*pause*]

DANNY: I think maybe I should go back to the reservation if you want me to get through high school. I could stay with Grandpa Joe.

TAG: Okay, sure, you can do that. But what happened to you? What happened at school? Talk to me!

DANNY: Who cut your hair off?

TAG: I did, Danny.

DANNY: Bullshit. You'd never cut it, you always said...

TAG: I cut it, Danny. Nobody else touched me. I swear.

DANNY: Why?

TAG: It's a different world in here, just trust me on this...

DANNY: I want to know.

TAG: I tell and you tell? All of it? Deal?

DANNY: ...Deal.

TAG: [*pause*] A couple of months back, a young kid gets transferred over here from the reformatory because he turned eighteen. He's Apache, a good-looking kid, but kind of small. He looks a little like you; I don't know, maybe every kid started looking like you after awhile. Anyway, King Con was going to turn him out, make him his punk. ...You know what I'm talking about?

DANNY: I know what you're talking about. Who's King Con?

TAG: A big guy, like almost seven feet tall, three hundred pound weightlifter. Triple murder, three lifes with no parole, nothing to lose. So they leave him alone. Everyone leaves him alone — guards, cons, everybody. He runs his own life.

DANNY: So where does your hair come into it?

130

TAG: Well, this kid got here right around the time your mom wrote me about you messing up. [DANNY *reacts, still defensive*] I looked at that kid and thought about you, thought about you in a place like this, about to be made into somebody's punk and maybe screwing up the whole rest of your life over it, maybe even getting killed over it. I kept looking at him, kept thinking about you, and finally I just couldn't let it happen. I couldn't do it. Just like if it really was you. How could I stand by and let a thing like that happen? How could I ever look at this kid's old man if I ever met him?

DANNY: What did you do?

TAG: Well, first I asked the Red Nation if they'd stand up for this kid. I figured if we all did, King Con would have to back off. But they wouldn't do it, because that's breaking the first rule of the convict code — you don't mess in another con's business. Ever.

DANNY: But he was messing in the kid's business...

TAG: It's complicated, Danny; I told you it's different in here. Anyway, I figured the Great Spirit was telling me, I'm on my own, I've got to stand on my own. Maybe because of how I fucked things up for you and your Mom, I don't know.

DANNY: So you cut your hair to fight him, so he couldn't grab your braid?

TAG: Nah, that's not it. No, what I did was, I prayed to the Great Spirit for you and your mom and Grandpa Joe to have a long life, then I neatened up my cell, and I walked over to his cell, and looked him straight in the eyes and told him that I couldn't let him turn that kid out because he reminded me of my only son.

131

DANNY: Were you afraid?

TAG: Sure. But I felt like a warrior, too. You know, it was all out in the open then, too late to back down by the time I looked into his eyes, and I felt like I was finally doing something real, after two years of sitting around feeling like a pile of garbage.

DANNY: What did he say?

TAG: When I stopped talking we just kept looking at each other for a long time. And then he says, "The boy is mine if I want him; you know that, don't you?" I said, "Yeah, I guess, but I would have to die first. I'm sorry."

DANNY: What were *you* sorry for? You weren't the one who was...

TAG: I was sorry, that's all. Like Grandpa Joe used to say, that all true warriors were sorry to have to go into battle. I know what he means now.

DANNY: You still had your hair, right?

TAG: Yeah, don't worry, I'm getting to it. Well, we kept looking in each other's eyes, and finally he said, "Are you telling me I can't, or are you asking me for a favor?" I realized that I hadn't even *asked* him not to do this thing. I had gone up to this guy and threatened him with me dying — which is a pretty stupid threat when you think about it — and I hadn't even just come out and asked him not to do this. So I said, "I'm asking you for a favor, with respect as your brother." And he said, "How long since you cut your hair?" I told him it's never been cut, and he said, "you'd give it up for your son?"

DANNY: Why? Why would he want your hair? Just to humiliate you?

TAG: No, not to humiliate me, just to keep his rep as the king. That's all. That's all he's got in this whole world, Danny. And he was giving me a chance to save the kid's ass without violence. He just needed to know I appreciated it — see, if King Con leaves this kid alone, nobody else can touch him either. That'd be like a personal insult. So this was a pretty big deal, and he needed some proof that I *took* it as a big deal. He's got my braid hung up there on his wall, and he respects me for giving it up.

DANNY: So the Apache kid is okay now?

TAG: Well, he's safe, that's all I know. I never have met him yet.

DANNY: What? Doesn't he know about what you did?

TAG: I don't know; doesn't really matter. What I did, I did it for me.

DANNY: [*pause*] Sounds like you did it for me.

TAG: I guess I did, yeah. ...Now it's your turn. What happened about you and school? [*no response*] Come on, we made a deal.

DANNY: [*reluctantly and softly*] Shit, dad. What do you think happened? I'm a drug dealer's son, that's what happened. [TAG *reacts, stunned and then ashamed*] After you went away, everybody started whispering about Danny's Dad this and Danny's Dad that, and my friends started saying their parents wouldn't let 'em hang out with me anymore, and the teachers too, the teachers acted like I was a doper, and they'd give me dirty looks whenever we'd have 'drug ed'... And they'd start giving me detentions for stuff I swear to God I didn't do, stupid stuff like somebody making a wisecrack in class, and they'd say it was me, and once a guy was caught with pot in his locker and they kept asking him if he got it from me, didn't he get it from Tag

Red Horse's kid? So what does mom want me to do, just keep taking all their shit? Just let 'em keep bad-mouthing you, and treating me like a fucking drug dealer?

TAG: Danny, I'm sorry...

DANNY: And she may not like the guys I hang out with now, but at least they're real friends. Fuck the school. Fuck the kids. Fuck the teachers. Fuck the whole fucking city!

[*a long, loud, unpleasant buzzer sounds offstage toward the end of* DANNY'S *line*]

TAG: Oh, shit! Shit!

DANNY: Do I have to go now?

TAG: [*utterly defeated*] One minute.

[*pause*]

DANNY: Dad, I haven't hurt nobody. The worst thing I did was, we knocked off a cigarette machine one time for some change for the arcade. I swear, I'm not into that kind of stuff. I won't do it again.

[TAG'S *hand gradually reaches out once again to the mesh*]

TAG: ...You know, if you did go finish school on the reservation, you'd be a couple hours closer to this place anyway.

DANNY: How often they let you get visitors?

TAG: Any weekend...*every* weekend.

DANNY: Yeah, I guess... I think the rez' is a good idea.

TAG: I'll bet Grandpa Joe might come see me if he had a ride up here.

DANNY: Yeah. I know he would.

[*Both doors open noisily*]

TAG: ...Danny, down to my bones, I'm sorry...

DANNY: [*getting up*] Dad, remember for my ninth birthday you took me on that cross-country run to Florida? And you bought me moccasins from that old Seminole lady with the real wrinkled face?

TAG: [*hand still on the mesh as he reluctantly starts to rise, looking over his shoulder toward the guards' door*] Yeah, I remember. And you wanted to drive; God, how you bugged me to drive. You couldn't even reach the gas pedal of that old Peterbilt, and you're bugging me to drive.

DANNY: I could reach it now.

[DANNY *moves toward exit,* TAG'S *hand still clinging to mesh as he calls*:]

TAG: Danny, I...

[DANNY *is gone, his door clangs shut*]

TAG: ...love you...

[TAG *turns and walks offstage as curtain falls.*]

the end

If you've enjoyed *Lineage And Other Stories*, please consider becoming a supporter of Human Kindness Foundation by buying copies of this and our other materials as gifts for friends and associates. Such sales help us continue sending these books free to inmates who request them. We spend no funds on advertising, so we rely on your enthusiasm and support.

This book and other materials are available directly from:

Human Kindness Foundation
PO Box 61619
Durham, NC 27715

www.humankindness.org